Light Enough to Float

LAUREN SEAL

Rocky Pond Books

ROCKY POND BOOKS
An imprint of Penguin Random House LLC, New York

First published in the United States of America by Rocky Pond Books,
an imprint of Penguin Random House LLC, 2024
Copyright © 2024 by Lauren Ellen Seal

Rocky Pond Books is a registered trademark and the colophon is a trademark
of Penguin Random House LLC.
The Penguin colophon is a registered trademark of Penguin Books Limited.

Visit us online at PenguinRandomHouse.com.

Library of Congress Cataloging-in-Publication Data is available.

ISBN 9780593700143
10 9 8 7 6 5 4 3 2 1

Printed in the United States of America
BVG

Design by Sylvia Bi
Text set in Museo Sans

FOR EVERYONE WHO LOVED ME THROUGH MY LOWS.
THIS BOOK AND I EXIST BECAUSE OF YOU.

AUTHOR'S NOTE

This book, though fiction, is inspired by my real-life struggles with anorexia, clinical depression, suicidal ideation, skin-picking, and anxiety. The character in this book suffers from the same disordered thinking and fatphobia I experienced as a teen and have spent half my life unlearning. If you struggle with any similar illnesses or thought patterns, this book may be emotionally taxing. If you need to put it down for weeks or months, know that is okay—the book will wait.

Not everyone's journey with an eating disorder or food-related illness will look like Evie's. Sadly, only a small percentage of individuals with eating disorders receive inpatient therapy. This can be for a variety of reasons, like socioeconomic status, privilege, and accessibility, but oftentimes it is because the individual does not meet the "typical" diagnostic criteria for an eating disorder. Anyone—regardless of physical size, race, age, and gender—can develop an eating disorder. I have done my best to represent a variety of patients.

At fourteen, all I wanted was for someone to tell me: *You are not alone. I have been where you are and made it out alive. You will survive this.* I read armfuls of books while hospitalized, searching for a story that mirrored my own serpentine recovery, but I never found it. This is the book my teenage self needed. Regardless of what drew you to it, I hope my book helps you realize how resilient and courageous you truly are. Remember: Your body—regardless of size or ability—is astonishing. You, dear reader, are astonishing. I see you, I see your struggle, and I am rooting for you.

SEPTEMBER

THE PSYCHIATRIST

dr. mantell,
the psychiatrist's
nameplate shouts.
i fight the urge
to ask if his name is
printed in loud uppercase
letters to drown out us
lowercase people and our
lowercase lives.

his scalpel-gray
eyes dissect me,
quarter me, sternum
to pelvis, left breast
        to right,
wrench me open, reach
inside, find all the
nothing
i've eaten since yesterday.

evie,
the muscles in my body contract
and freeze. i sit, still and staring:

portrait of a girl afraid.

evie,
do you know why you're here?

WHY I'M HERE

because of the tests.

they took my height and weight,
took my blood, took my heart
rate, took my pee,
took my family history,
then a man in a lab coat took
my parents aside
to tell them i failed.

i've never failed a test in my life.

because my mother says
this is an important
appointment. we are lucky
a cancellation let
capital-*t* Them
fit me in.

because sometimes
i get a little sad and overwhelmed.
because sometimes i feel
like falling asleep and never waking up.

because my parents and my sister and my friend darcy and my dog would probably be happier without me. because all i do is try and try to be a perfect daughter and sister and friend and student and person but it doesn't make me any less scared of living. because i would be happier without me.

because sometimes
i have trouble
eating
and my mother and i
argue over dinner plates
        just three more bites
like i'm a misbehaving toddler.

i slouch down in my chair,
glare at the doctor,
refuse to speak.

WHY I'M REALLY HERE

because of my lies.

the first:
        i'm on a diet.
wrong,
i've been on all of them:
mediterranean,
keto,
raw food,
low-fat,
gluten-free,
atkins,
vegan,
paleo,
south beach.
whatever let me
restrict.
intermittent eating with frequent fasting.

second:
        it's only one more . . .
sit-up,
push-up,
squat,
mile.

that i wouldn't add
one
plus
one
plus
one
plus
one
            until
my muscles ached,
body broke.

third:
i'm in control.
i can stop whenever
i want.

PROFESSIONAL OPINION

your height and weight
are very low
for a fourteen-year-old,

dr. mantell says

same with your hemoglobin,
and your electrolytes.
you have all the symptoms of
extreme malnourishment.

pride flutters in my chest.

i nod along benignly, glare
at the office door my mom
stands behind. i missed school
to be here. does no one
care about my GPA?

the results from your EKG
indicate
bradycardia.

bradycardia?

a slow heart rate.
thirty-eight beats per minute.

i nod. i don't want him
to think i am a stupid girl.
i am not a stupid girl.

do you understand?
don't blink.
yes.

evie,
your heart is so slow
it could stop
at any moment.

the offbeat drumming of said organ
floods my ears.
dr. mantell observes my reaction.
me the frog, his eyes
the scalpel. see the ease
with which they slit
my pale, white skin,
my muscles,
my rib cage,
until my empty guts
spill out.

you are,
in my professional opinion,
anorexic.

THAT WORD

anorexic.
it lodges itself
in my coronary artery.
heart palpitates. thousands
of excuses
dam up my mouth:
i eat,
i'm fat,
i'm not obsessed with my looks,
i eat,
that's not the type of girl i am.
i come from a good family—

but i eat,
i squeak.

do you eat enough?

i think about
the ice cream i don't eat.
the chocolate,
the potato chips
i also don't eat.

the avocados,
bananas,
cookies,
french fries,
granola,
hamburgers,
marshmallows,
peanut butter,
spaghetti,
tacos,
yogurt,
an alphabet of off-limits food.

yes?

dr. mantell leans back in his chair,
scrunches his white face in thought,
impatiently *tap-tap-taps* his pen against
the notes he's been taking.

> *i think we should get*
> *your mother in here.*

MY MOTHER

she barges in
with as much restraint
as a freight train. this woman
who gobbles firewood
so she can keep
running and running and
running along
her one-track mind.

my diagnosis derails her.
she fires coal-hot questions:
> *what does this mean?*
> *how does she get better?*
> can *she get better?*
> *what about her heart?*
> *how do i make her gain weight?*

i think she's really asking,
> *what do i do*
> *with this damaged daughter?*

DROWNING

mom and dr. mantell
position me as a
problem
to solve.
say words like
program,
therapy,
refeeding.
i'm stuck on
anorexic,
ANorexIC,
ANOREXIC.

it floods me, fills my lungs.
i can't shout, can't breathe,
only flail. fail.

drown.
too weak to
surface.

I'VE DROWNED BEFORE

when i was five, at a beach
that's more dream than memory.
bubble-gum-ice-cream-blue sky,
chocolate-brown lake.
i ran, reckless,
into calf-deep water.
splashed in waves left
in motorboats' wakes.
another girl, eight or nine,
joined me, chanted,

>   *follow me, follow me,*
>   *i will lead, so follow me!*

powerless against
this pied piper,
i followed, the water
reaching my shoulders,
my neck, my scalp.
i followed, until I couldn't.
my feet floundered
for lake bottom.
my left foot found
ground. stepped
down and sunk, stuck
in deep muck.

scared, limbs swinging,
i struggled, stomped,
trapped my right foot.
panic pounded
in violent waves.

                         come on,
my new friend giggled.
my head barely breached
the surface.
restless ripples
muffled my screams.
help!

only silence answered.

my last thought as
static clouded in:
this is all my fault.

warm hands grabbed
under my armpits.
hauled so hard
my side-body ached.
                    evie! you know the rule,
                    don't go in past your waist!
my dad hissed through
gritted teeth.

he carried me
to safety,
where my rules have kept me
ever since.

GASPING

i clung to my rules;
tried to be
a good girl,
a smart girl,
an abiding girl.
ended up here gasping
for air around
mouthfuls of my own
excruciating
perfection.

HABITS

on the drive home
i scratch my scalp until
it bleeds. until fingernails
and dirty blond roots are coated
red with relief
and half-healed scabs.

mom taps my knee
with her pale hand.
        evie,
        no picking.

i stop
at mom's request.

        aren't you excited?
        this could be the help we need
        to get you into recovery.

i smile out of habit,
not happiness.

I CAN'T

by the time we get home
the prickling, tickling itch
of my scalp has moved
into my veins.

i can't sit still, i can't sit still, i can't sit still.

i race to my room, already
halfway upstairs when
mom announces,
            i'm going out for cigarettes.

i burst through the door.
implode.
convulse like a fish caught
on a line,
trapped and dying.
i must be dying.

my faulty heart hammers
the walls of my chest.
i'm scared it will burst.
i'm scared it will stop.
i try to breathe, but only
choke, gag.

i can't breathe. i can't breathe. i'm anorexic.
can't breathe. wish i could breathe. anorexic.
i can't breathe and i'm anorexic and i'm going to die.

COMFORT

harlow, my giant
portuguese water dog,
nudges open my door,
creeps cautiously closer,
snuffles behind my ear
with his wet black nose.

he curls his body
around mine, big spoon
to little spoon. rests
his chin on my rib cage.

i reach shaky hands
to stroke his soft head.
he inhales, lets out
a slow sigh. i copy
his breathing for as long
as it takes
to feel strong.
i love you, harlow.

he huffs, which means

i love you too,
you sad, silly girl.

AVOIDANCE

when my mom
returns, i'm collapsed
on the couch, tv blaring,
phone out, scrolling
instagram,
harlow huddled
against me.
i've splashed my blanched
face with freezing water,
massaged swollen bags
from under my tired eyes.

she knits her eyebrows.
>   *you look awful.*
>   *are you okay?*
as if we both don't know
the answer.

she carries a plastic bag
from the pharmacy, so full
it's bulging. a pack
of toothpaste peeks
out the top.
why'd it take thirty minutes
to buy cigarettes down the street?

her hazel eyes darken,
jaw sets, she turns away.
      they were out
      of the kind i like.

if you say so.

she and the plastic bag
shuffle away.

pretty sure avoidance
is an inherited trait.

CASUALTY

avoiding food
is an art form
i've perfected.
when i'm surrounded
by schoolwork, seated with
laptop open, headphones in,
mom forgets to check
if i've eaten.

my phone vibrates
with a text from my
best friend—only friend—
darcy.

> *where r u?*
> *this class sucks.*

my stomach drops
like on a roller coaster.
i've perfected
avoiding darcy, too.
because hanging out
means popcorn at movies,
fast food dates,
trips to 7-eleven for
candy and slushies.

constant questions
about why
i'm not
eating.

i type:
sorry, sick.
be back soon.
hit send.

ONE BIG HAPPY

serenaded by clinking cutlery
and the syncopated sounds
of chewing, i examine my chicken
thigh, imagine i'm slicing
my own as i cut
off a sliver. would my body
smell similar
      if cooked?
would my own white,
boneless, skinless
flesh
      be as tender?
wedge itself in my teeth,
make my gums
      tickle?

      the doctor said
      evie is anorexic,
mom announces,
      just like i thought.

i choke on the chicken
mom watches me nibble
out the corner of her eye.

dad asks,

> *are you sure*
> *it's not just a sensitive stomach?*

> *peter, she's skin and bones!*

my sister, wren, smirks.

> *hear that?*
> *you look terrible, evie.*

i stick out my tongue,
wren opens her mouth wide,
displaying a dissection
of half-chewed chicken and peas.
i gag.

mom gapes like i've
puked all over
the table. she turns
and glares
at dad, as if to say:
is this not proof our daughter
is dying before our eyes?

dad pushes up his glasses,
rubs his face so hard
his cream skin turns pink.
wren's eyes roll. she cuts

her chicken into chunks,
mixes in mashed potatoes,
peas,
gravy.
a slop of excess.
i grit my teeth,
study my plate,
      orderly,
        nothing touching.

dad sighs.
              well, cleo,
              what do you want me to do?

      help me
      support evie.
      we can get through this.
      as a family.

if my stomach weren't
so full,
i would laugh.

IMPOSTERS

we collide in the bathroom
doorway, wren and i,
dance.
                    i duck to my right,
she dives to her left,
i sidestep left,
                    she sashays right.
until i, on instinct,
freeze.

her eyes, identical
to our mother's,
sever me, head
to bloated belly.
unease crawls
up my neck
with frozen fingers.

                    so, anorexic?
yep.

i almost tell her
i'm scared. explain how
i followed the rules,
how those rules twisted

and grew into thorny vines
that impale me
whenever i breathe. but
                    that's not me.

good night.

harlow trails behind,
the pads of his feet echoing
in the hallway along with
everything unsaid. i almost swear
wren's eyes start tearing. but
                    that's not her.

i shut my door.
pray we're
more ourselves
tomorrow.

GUARD DOG

harlow sleeps
at my feet, snout facing
the door. my protector
from the monsters
lurking.

PEST

i can't find
my favorite baggy
sweatshirt or half my underwear
and socks, leaving me with
stained, period-only panties
(that i haven't needed
for months)
and the blue sweater
that clings to my gut.

i moan at my reflection,
adjust the sweater
wrinkles until
they fall in just the right
way to cover my fat.

like a ghost,
wren's pale face pops up
behind me in the mirror.

*i can't believe you get to
miss school again. i wish
i was the crazy one with
all the appointments.*

i whip around.
what are you doing in here?
get out of my room.

wren flips her eyelids
inside out and waggles
her tongue. i gag,
like she wanted.

you're so gross.
i said get out!
i grab a pillow
from my bed, throw it
as she slams
the door.

i breathe a sigh
of relief. at least
wren is back to normal.

WISHFUL THINKING

dad's busy with work
so lucky me
i'm stuck with mom
chattering away
      about hospitals,
      food,
      recovery,
for the forty-five-minute drive
back into the city.

my forehead bounces
against the cool glass
of the passenger-side car
window, turns itchy, then tender
from constant impact.
i imagine a pit opening,
molten lava devouring
      the highway,
      vehicles,
      me.

what are you thinking about?

nothing.

CRAZY

can you take yourself up
while i pay for parking?

i drag the rubber soles
of my sneakers across
the linoleum floor.
squeak my way
to the elevators,
join the crush of visitors,
patients, and doctors elbowing
their way inside.

every bit of my body
touches the body
of someone else.
i pull myself in close,
shrink.
an old man squeezes
into my space, touches
my fat arm, my fat
leg. shrugs with a little
what-can-you-do smile.
i clench my lips
to communicate back
i-feel-uncomfortable-with-my-body-being-in-

physical-contact-with-another-human.
i-feel-uncomfortable-with-my-body-being.

the bell dings for
the second floor. doors
open. a press of people
exit. more enter. i bite
my tongue, count
seconds before the next
ding. third
floor. the doors slide
open. cool air
rushes in, i rush
out. check that no one
is watching,
slowly slink
toward the
psychiatric wing.

i don't want people thinking
i'm crazy or anything.

SPLINTERING

the patients wandering the halls
outside dr. mantell's office
look knotted with hunger:
        eyes sunken hollows,
        cheekbones like knives,
        papier-mâché skin
        wrapped around bones.
how i wish
i appeared.

i seat myself in one of three stiff
chairs. suck my stomach in,
hide its folds from the others.
turn my gaze
to my lap,
        my own
        white-knuckled fists.

in minutes, pain
bruises my butt cheeks.
i squirm, search for a position
to relieve the ache
in my tailbone.
i glance toward the unit

doors, eyes hunting
for mom. above me,
fluorescent lights buzz
mosquito-like. my scalp itches.
i claw at crusted wounds.

mom charges in,
        stiff-legged,
        jaw clenched,
a woman ready for war.
her neck quivers.
her eyes are
        red-rimmed,
        mascara smudged.
she doesn't meet my gaze.
stares past me
as she nears.

i stand on tiptoes,
stretch my neck,
lean into her line
of vision. her eyes
flicker away.
she will not
look at
me.

she halts
four feet away,

hands trembling as she sets
a purple suitcase
at her feet.

mom?
two nurses block
the exit. double doors crash,
the bolt catching with
a deafening clunk.

the other patients
scurry away, scared
of being caught
in the teeth of this
betrayal.

my heart splinters.
mom, please.

. . .

she's
abandoning
me
         here?

WINDED

mom dries her eyes
on her sweater cuff.

>   *you didn't give me a choice.*
>   *you're too sick.*
>   *we can't fix*
>   *this alone.*

her words wind me,
punch breath from my lungs.
leave me
          wheezing.
yet she's the one who buckles
forward, opens her empty mouth,
releases a
          keening cry.

my body quakes.
i stick my tongue
between my teeth, quiet
their clatter. bury
trembling hands
in legging pockets.

take a breath, hold it.
clench fists, eyes, body
tighttighttighttighttighttighttighttighttighttighttight.
swallow my feelings
deep into my belly
       where all unwanted things go.

hobble to mom, drape
her in my arms.
it's okay, mom.
it'll be okay.

DR. MANTELL

the nameplate
yells and yells and yells and yells and yells and yells.
i read it
over and over and over and over and over and over
and over
as i
drown
drown
drown
drown
drown
drown
drown.

PRECISELY WHY

dr. mantell pulls bmi
charts, circles my weight
from yesterday. draws
another circle above
the line that signifies
"normal."

> under our care,
> evie will gain
> twenty pounds.

bile burns my throat.
twenty pounds!

he does not acknowledge
me. i wipe my sweaty, shaking
palms on the vinyl
chair. leave a slick
trail of perspiration.

> we'll gradually rehydrate her.
> feed her four meals a day,
> with incremental caloric
> increases. she'll receive group
> and one-on-one therapy.

i'll start her on a course of
anti-depressants, as well
as vitamins and an
antacid, for indigestion.
she will be constantly
supervised by our
trained staff.

mom's chair creaks
as she leans forward.
    this all sounds perfect.

i'm five again, trapped
underwater, swaying,
unable to breathe.
no.
i'll look like a whale.

    evie, enough.
mom isn't used to
her perfect girl
saying no.

dr. mantell
does not blink.

    this isn't a discussion.
    you're very sick, evie.
    this is how you get better.

no.

i don't want to do it.

                                                 of course you don't.

                                                 that's precisely why you're here.

IMPRISONED

dr. mantell clasps
an orange band
around my wrist.

loose enough that my
circulation
isn't cut off. tight
enough that it won't slip
off past my knuckles,
though I try.

a cool, plastic shackle.

this tells security
you're on close watch
and not allowed
to leave.

LUCKY ME

with a squeak of the office
door a nurse enters. she's about
mom's age, black, a sympathetic
smile softening her face.
i focus on that, instead of
her long, ropey body—
effortlessly thin, like
mine will never be.

tammy, can you show evie
to her room?

my muscles lock tighter
than the unit's metal doors.
i refuse to stand.
mom gently pulls at my arm.
evie, come on.
i do not move.
the next tug
is rougher.
evie, don't make this harder.
listen to dr. mantell.

what am i, if not
a good girl,

a smart girl,
an abiding girl?

my knees creak
as i stand. i am
a wooden marionette,
other people's expectations
my strings.

i let tammy lead me
and mom to my room.
it smells of chemicals
and burnt plastic.
contains two hospital beds, striped
curtains for "privacy." beside each bed,
a side table and vinyl chair.
two closets.
one shared bathroom.

perfect. maybe
me and my roommate
can stay up late
swapping secrets.
have ourselves a morbid
little slumber party.

                         lucky you,
nurse tammy chirps,

                         you get the window.

the window that doesn't open,
reinforced with steel wire,
and overlooks a small courtyard,
a parking lot,
a mcdonald's.
right. lucky me.

ABANDONED

mom stutters awkward
goodbyes once tammy leaves.

>   *your father will visit after*
>   *work. he'll bring anything*
>   *i forgot to pack. let the nurses*
>   *know if you want a favorite*
>   *sweater or something?*

she sways toward me. stops.
pulls her hands
close to her sides.
>   *i should go.*
>   *i love you,*
>   *you know.*

not sure i do know.
i don't say it back.

IV THERAPY

nurse tammy returns,
iv pole rattling behind her.

                                    an iv for evie,

she singsongs,
smiling like an idiot.

                                    let's get you sitting
                                    down for this.

i do as i'm told. fall
on the edge of the bed.
rubber tubing is wrapped
tightly around my bicep.
i wince as the rubber pulls
baby hairs from my skin.

                                    can you make a fist
                                    for me, please?

i curl my hand,
imagine i'm about to punch
dr. mantell's stupid face.
tammy *tap-tap-tap-taps*
my wrist, grimaces.

these veins are
too tiny. i'll have to use the ones
in your elbow.
take a deep breath for me.
1 . . . 2 . . . 3 . . .

my skin dimples around
the needle point,
splits with a sharp pinch.
an inch of needle slowly disappears
under my pasty skin.
rubber tourniquet removed,
i bend my elbow. the needle
squirms like a parasite in my vein.

tammy hooks my body
to the machine.
with a press of buttons
potassium pumps into me,
stings my veins with bitter cold.
i bite my cheek,
do not let myself
cry.
         not yet.
         not when i'm being watched.

THE GRAND TOUR

are you ready for your tour?
i glare. tammy's bright voice
at odds with my bleak life.
i shuffle behind her, grasp
the iv pole, its faulty wheel
chirping like a starving bird.

the unit is one big rectangle,
like a big box.
or a cage.

the unit is white and sterile.
bleached. the air heavy
with disinfectant that irritates
my nose, leaves me on
the edge of a sneeze.

tammy points out the unit's selling features:
five patient rooms,
dietitian's office,
psychologists' office,
meal room,
weight room,
medication room,
laundry room,
lounge, and

dr. mantell's office.

the nurses' desk, directly
across from my room,
is the hub of
the unit's wheel. they can
scan the hallway, and me,
with a few steps, perked ears,
a nosy flick of the wrist.

during the tour we pass
patients sleeping, pacing,
watching. their hungry eyes
judging. they do not say hello.

they take a while
to warm to new admissions.

i hunch lower, hide.

and that's your new home!
any questions?

can you kill me now
and get it over with?

i inhale deeply, paste
a practiced, polite smile
on my face.
can i go
unpack my bags?

RUMPLED

i return to my room
in a daze
and find a new nurse—
      white with graying hair
       and eyeglasses that highlight
       wrinkles and bags—
elbows deep in my suitcase
like she owns it.

anger hatches in my chest,
scuttles through my body
on tiny spider legs.
what are you doing?
those are my things!

she removes a razor.
             prohibited.

my mom packed that.
this is my stuff.
you can't go through it like that.

            unit rules
            state otherwise.

she stares down her nose,

a disapproving teacher.
or prison guard.
waves my pink razor in my face,
the three metallic blades
mocking me with a glint.

> *i will not tolerate patients*
> *sneaking in contraband.*

i didn't—

> *this will be locked*
> *in the medication room.*

then she reaches out
an arm, wiggles her
fingers in a "gimme"
motion.

> *your phone will be locked*
> *up as well.*

i gape
like she just asked
me for a kidney.
what?

> *your phone.*
> *it's prohibited.*
> *we can't have you*
> *scrolling through*

dangerous sites.

but how will i
talk to people?

                    with the patient phone.
                    now hand it over.

i extract my phone
from my leggings,
take one last look
at my lock screen—
harlow, rolling in
a patch of grass, smiling.
the screen goes black
as i power it off, hand it
to my captor.

she walks away, head high,
shoes clacking a smug
rhythm. i hold back hot tears,
bury my head in my suitcase,
inhale the smell of harlow's
fur, laundry detergent,
vanilla body lotion.
home.

mouth smothered
by rumpled clothes,
i scream.

1200

the stench of meat
rolls in like fog.
bile burns the back
of my throat. my mouth
used to water at the greasy
smell of cheese
melting on pizza. now,
the scent of food
turns my stomach.

tammy's head pops out
from around the curtain
i've pulled closed.

> *hi evie. it's dinner time.*
> *i'll walk you to the meal room.*

i follow, iv wheel chirping.

> *sit down, i'll find*
> *your tray for you.*

i perch at the table nearest
the door. look at anything
except the other patients
beside me. the meal room
is plastered in handwritten signs.

rules printed in neat,
colorful marker:
> "food need not be red hot."
> "no mixing of foods."
> "no over-seasoning."
> "all uneaten calories
> will be replaced with ensure."
> "remember: a calorie is a calorie is a calorie."

tammy plunks a plastic-wrap-covered
tray in front of me. taped to it
is a piece of paper with my name,
and a number. 1200.
1200 calories
every. single. day.

dread clenches my stomach
into a fist. i grip the warm plastic
wrap, lift it, unleash a cloud
of condensation.
reveal a mound of meatloaf,
buttered baked potato,
steamed carrots.

i can't eat this.
i look toward tammy, but
the gray-haired nurse answers instead.

> *you can't leave until you finish.*

but ma'am . . .

                        darlene.

darlene,
i'll be sick.

                      eat it or drink meal replacement.
                      your choice.

the only thing worse than eating
calories is drinking them.
ask any diet influencer.

one nurse blocks
the doorway, the others
circle the tables, vultures
prepared to swoop
at the slightest sign of scraps.
hands shaking, i shovel
a spoonful of carrots into
my mouth. chew and chew.
don't think about the pounds.
the carrots turn to mush.

repeat.

NO EXCUSES

darlene double-checks my plate.

what's this?

she points to a lonely forkful
of meatloaf.

you must eat everything.

i'm too full.
my stomach hurts.

no excuses.

she marches away, returns
with a shot glass of thick, brown
ensure. shoves it in my face.

drink.

what?

drink your leftover calories.

my face flares hot,

but the good girl in me
cannot rebel.
i clutch the glass. sip.
chocolate.
of course it tastes
like goddamn chocolate.

she watches, one eyebrow raised.
i scrunch my eyes shut,
down the liquid
in one great gulp.

darlene inspects the glass
for any missed drops
before dismissing me.

i lurch back to my room,
the contents of my stomach
sloshing.

BREAKDOWN

i need to escape
from the nurses, this place,
       my body.

i pull and pull my bathroom door
until my roommate walks in,
sits on the other bed.
she is a porcelain doll—
delicate, inches shorter
than me, milky white skin
hidden under layers
of wavy red hair.

> *they lock the bathrooms after we eat,*
> *so we can't purge. if you need to go,*
> *i can ask a nurse to come supervise.*
> *i'm candace, by the way.*

i drop my hands, stare at the
speckled floor. a child caught
in a tantrum.

> *are you okay?*
> *do you want me to grab someone?*

i shake my head, pull the curtains
around my bed. curl up tight.

listen to the potassium drip of the iv.

realizing conversation is hopeless,
candace leaves our room, her slippers
slapping linoleum as she exits.

i grab the fat of my stomach. my body
soft as play-doh, oozing out of my
leggings. i'm a mess of mass,
blubbering on the bed.

DIDN'T THINK

dad stops by
after evening snack.
in his arms:
> my purple quilt,
> books and binders,
> a stuffed dog that looks
> like harlow.

he peeks at the iv pole,
pumping and plumping me.
swallows hard, rests his glasses
on his pale forehead, rubs his eyes,
falls on my bed,
and cries.

i shift, uneasy. i want
to leave. i want to
tell him to stop.
instead, i sit
at the foot of the bed,
lean against him.

his arms hover around me,
too scared to hug.
he gives up his attempt

in seconds.

i'm so sorry.
i didn't think anything
was wrong.

it's okay, dad.
i didn't either.

EVENING SYMPHONY

harlow's bedtime snores
are replaced by
my roommate's whistling
breath. my iv pump beats
like a mechanical heart.

a loudspeaker blares with
a male voice announcing:
> *code blue,*
> *unit 4g3*
> *code blue,*
> *unit 4g3,*
> *code blue,*
> *unit 4g3.*

when i do sleep,
it's light. troubled.
i dream i'm home, lying
on the ground. harlow
bolting out the front door,
onto the busy street.
his panicked barks are loud,
but i'm too weak to move.
i call for him as he runs away,
my anemic voice echoing
in an empty room.

SLAUGHTER

my morning begins with lines:
the line
        outside the med room,
the lines
        of my iv being flushed
        and reattached,
the line
        of patients waiting
        to be weighed.

the weight room runs
with the efficiency
of a slaughterhouse.
everyone standing single
file, eyes forward. one after
the other, they disappear
into the room, into the metallic
scrape and clunk
of weights and balances.
exit on trembling legs,
faces drawn and bloodless.

                    next.

the room is bare.
a sink,

two chairs,
the scale.

remove your shoes and
step onto the scale.

the cold platform wobbles,
gives under my feet.
an unwelcome reminder
that my body weighs anything.
the nurse fiddles with buttons.
the scale beeps.
the digital face displays
my weight and i see
how much of me
i still have left
to lose.

A CALORIE IS A CALORIE

the rest of the morning is filled
with appointments.

first, with dr. mantell.
he reiterates my treatment
plan, tells me nothing new.
i hold my breath
until my lungs are bloated
with frustration.
how soon can i go home?

                    the earliest i'll even consider
                    is thirty days, and that depends
                    on your health.

thirty. i cling to the number.
i can pretend i'm healthy
for that long.

i'm then directed to the unit's
dietitian. her office walls
covered in food pyramids,
pictures of portioned plates,
and signs proclaiming all food
is good food. she shows me

how to select meals
from premade,
preapproved menus.
                you can choose your favorite foods.
my favorite food
is no food.
she tries convincing me
eating 300 calories worth
of cake is the exact same
as eating 300 calories
worth of broccoli,
repeats the phrase
"a calorie is a calorie is a calorie"
at least ten times.
a mantra. a lie.
i tune her out.

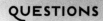

QUESTIONS

my last appointment
is with the psychologist,
a gentle-voiced, east indian woman
who introduces herself as anna.
i stare at her office fish
tank, at the bloated body
of the bottom feeder.
answer stupid questions like

> *did you have a happy childhood?*
> *is there a family history of*
> *mental illness?*
> *have you ever wanted to hurt yourself?*

yes.
some.
no.

but i scratch at my scalp,
scrape away old scabs,
relief rushing through me
as my fingernails
dampen with blood.

I DIDN'T KNOW

even in here school still
occurs. in the afternoon,
a block of two hours
that won't interfere with meals.
only two other patients are
young enough to attend.
one of them is a boy.

i scuffle behind him
as a nurse escorts us off unit.
he's lanky and stooped, arms
too long for the rest of his body,
skin as pasty as the mashed
potatoes served at lunch.

i didn't know boys
could have eating disorders.

THE WITCH AND THE WOLFMAN

the hospital school
is a single room bursting
with color and clutter:
>rainbow desks,
>mismatched chairs,
>congested bookshelves,
>an old chalkboard,
>a row of computers,
>and posters everywhere.

a witch and a wolfman
talk noisily in
the middle of the space.
the witch is dressed in earthy linens,
bangles adorning any bare
speck of light flesh. the wolfman
towers, his shirtsleeves
not quite reaching his forearms,
thick, curly hair growing
from every olive pore.

wide smiles open their
faces when they see me.

>*our new student!*

the witch screams,
flying forward.

> *my name is jean coots, and this*
> *large, handsome man is alfred elliot.*
> *call us jean and alfred.*

she grabs my hand, guides me
to a seat between her and alfred.

> *tell us a bit about yourself.*

the boy and girl who
joined me bury their heads
in binders. i try to
speak but my tongue is too
big for my mouth. i trip
over syllables, manage
a stilted reply.

my name's evie.
i like school.
i've got a 4.0 gpa?

alfred clears his throat,
speaks in a voice
gentler than his size would suggest.

> *we try not to focus*
> *on grades here. we'll*
> *keep caught up*

with your regular school,
but you need to
concentrate on your
recovery. your health
is more important.

there's a slight edge to his voice,
as if he suspects i'll disagree
with what he says.
which i do,
but have enough sense
not to tell him.

GHOST

for two days, the nurses
leave me to hide
in my room, crying
and pinching my fat.
i tattoo my body
in stinging
red fingerprints.

after my first night
my white-wristband-wearing,
allowed-off-unit
roommate, candace,
also leaves me alone.
i'm young, sick,
undeserving of her
attention.

she avoids looking
at me when she walks
to the bathroom, despite
having to pass my bed.
she pretends i am a ghost.
i wish i were, wish
my body were
light enough
to float.

WELCOME

on thursday, nasty
darlene drags me
from my perch
on the shallow window
ledge, her brittle nails digging
into my forearm. i don't
complain, scared
she will make me eat
more food. she forces
me to follow her to
the patient lounge
for the group session
she's leading.

i am greeted by eight
anxious faces. the patients'
eyes slither over my body,
weigh my worth by the width
of my legs, the bulge of my
breasts. discomfort crawls
up my spine.

a patient across the room—
a halo of wispy blond hair
sprouting from her head
like poplar fluff—pats the seat

of the empty recliner beside her.

darlene glares as I smile
and sit, her stare set
on me a few seconds
too long.

>   *because this is evie's first group*
>   *we will start with introductions.*

the other patients rattle off
their names and diagnoses
like army ranks:

carson, the lone teenage boy,
face pale as an eggshell,
anorexic and bulimic.

marianne, the other teen patient,
her glossy black skin
hidden by a veil of braids.
anorexic.

candace, my too-perfect
porcelain-skinned roommate,
who proudly states she is trans.
anorexic and bulimic.

kristy, her soft, tanned curves
sticking out among

the forest of emaciated limbs,
anorexic and bulimic. relapsed.

esther, brown knuckles
so scabbed and scarred
they look like ground beef.
bulimic. relapsed.

nadia, asian, her posture
as perfect as a dancer.
anorexic.

tabitha, eyes half-shut
with sleep. she introduces
herself first as cree,
then bulimic. relapsed.

beside me, jayda,
the white pixie woman
with the halo of hair,
anorexic and bulimic.
multiple relapses.
three admissions.
          third time's the charm, right?

they are all older, more
attractive than me.
darlene clears her throat,
a signal for me to speak.

evie.
anorexic. i guess.

darlene rolls her eyes.
>*now that that's over,*
>*on to our topic—*
>*laxative abuse.*

jayda leans toward me,
the warmth of her bare arm
seeping through my sweater.
>*welcome to the shithole, evie.*

NEW RULES

the rules of the unit
are written in absolutes.
i must either

do nothing
no hiding food
no purging
no numbers talk
no cutting
no exercise
no stairs
no phone
no leaving

or everything
eat all my food
take all my meds
attend all therapy
gain all the weight

one extreme
or the other. no room
for moderation. my rules,
but flipped.

WHEN I BROKE

i became fat at twelve.
when puberty hit me
like a semitruck,
so did the weight.

the smooth terrain of my skin
reddened and cratered.
i picked at pimples until
they bled, cried over
the scabs crusting my face.

the tarry brown blood
of my first period
signaled something sinister.
my hips and breasts
rounded, softened, my stomach peeked
over the tops of pants. my arms
and thighs rippled with every step.
this new body so unlike the
tall, tanned, and taut girls
i followed on instagram.

luckily, the internet is full
of ways to fix what's broken.
tips for tightening, lessons

on lessening. six sure-fire
steps for a sexy stomach.

diet and exercise posts
became the one thing
i happily ate up.

ROOTED

the unit's four square
meals a day hurt
going down. the corners cut
my throat, tear my trachea,
stab my stomach.

already, my body expands around
food like a tree, grows in rings
from the inside out. i worry
my limbs will bow under
fatty foliage. that my body
will grow roots, sink—immovable—
into the earth.

MAKESHIFT

i try to detach. but it's
like duct tape on a screen
door. real life forces itself in.

FINE FINE FINE

i illicitly log in
to instagram
on the school computer
and darcy's worried messages
appear like an accusation.

*hey evie, u weren't
in school.
where r u?*

*ur not answering
any of my texts.*

*it's been a couple
days. r u ok?*

*i'm rlly worried.
can u message me
back or call so i
no ur ok?*

*i called ur house
and ur mom told
me u were in the
hospital??
what's going on???*

the flimsy film of detachment
tears. i cannot tell her why
i'm here. she won't understand.
she'll think i'm pathetic.
she'll hate me. she'll stop
being my friend.

i peck out a reply.
i'm fine.
everything is fine.
i'll be back soon.

i'm fine.
everything is fine.
i'm fine.
everything is fine.
everything.

A FRIEND

i log out, sit at my desk,
ignore the tickle
in the roof of my mouth
that means tears. ignore
carson and marianne.
open my book. break.
bawl over a yellowing
copy of *animal farm.*
the room quiets, aside
from my sobs. i grab
my hood, fold it over
my pitiful face, and hide.

behind me are the soft,
slow steps of someone
approaching a skittish hare.
a warm hand rubs circles
on my back, the scent of
spearmint signaling it's jean.
she gathers me up, grabs
my notes, guides me into
a windowless office
barely bigger than a closet.

i curl up snail-shell tight

on a plastic chair, hide
my face, dig my nails into my knees.

are you okay, evie?

i shake my head.
no.
everything's wrong.

what's everything?

me.
being here.

i wipe my nose on the sleeve
of my oversized sweater,
leave a smear of snot
behind. i suppress a gag.
jean slides a box
of tissues toward me
and my face blazes.

all our students go through
an adjustment period.

i don't want to adjust,
i want to go home.

she creaks open

a desk drawer,
removes a swath
of lined paper.

> *write down how you're feeling.*
> *get those emotions out*
> *and somewhere safe.*

i have schoolwork.

jean lifts my syllabus,
tears it in half with a loud
rip i feel in my chest.
the room tilts. my stomach
churns, my jaw goes weak.
she continues until the paper
is nothing but confetti, tosses it up,
lets it rain down around us.

> *orwell is overdone.*
> *your only assignment today*
> *is to write.*

but . . .

she grins.
> *get started, evie,*
> *it's for a grade.*

TORRENT

scared
fat   lonely
abandoned

                        fat
                unlovable
        angry
fat   not good enough
fat fat fat fat fatfatfatfatfat

i scrawl it in light, looping letters,
faint, then dark, hard. the words
devolve into scribbles. the pages
become as messy as i feel.
then the paper   rips
from pressure.

chills run up my body.
i drop the pencil. sit up
straight. still.

jean watches, unfazed,
a sad smile on her lips.
        well, it's a start.

COMPULSIVE BOREDOM

weekends on the unit
are worse than the week.
no school, no jean.
i stay in my room,
curtains drawn, candace
pointedly ignoring me.
my iv drips in time with
the second hand of the clock.
i clench my glutes and abs for
five iv drips, unclench for three.
repeat for hours.

ONE WEEK

monday marks a week
since my diagnosis.
five new pounds sit
on me like a winter
coat i cannot wait
to shed.

after breakfast, jayda
finds me pacing the hall
iv wheel cheeping
like an angry squirrel.

> *i'm gonna take a guess*
> *and say you had your first*
> *big weight increase?*

mortification
stops my steps.
is it that noticeable?
i ask, arms crossing
to cover my belly.

> *god no. you look the same.*
> *i meant the walking.*
> *i do it too, when*

my weight jumps.
try to burn what i can.

i gaze at the ground, mutter,
that's not what i'm doing
though it absolutely is
what i'm doing.

jayda smirks,
kicks the wheels
of my iv pole.
>   *maybe hold off*
>   *until you're unhooked*
>   *from your boyfriend here.*
>   *you know what they say:*
>   *the squeaky wheel*
>   *gets extra ensure.*

would the nurses do that?
barely concealed
horror shakes
my voice.

she laughs,
>   *who knows?*
>   *but seriously,*
>   *don't worry.*
>   *whatever you've gained*
>   *is water weight. it'll even*

out when the iv is gone.

i make a silent
vow to not drink
water outside mealtimes.

SHARDS

i call home on
the gray patient phone.
it's set in a small alcove,
providing the illusion
of privacy.

mom picks up on
the third ring.
     hello?

hi mom. it's me.

     evie!
my name turns to a sob
she attempts to cover
with a cough.
     how are you doing?

i'm in a hospital.
so, yeah, not great.

     it's been hard here too.
     did you want to talk to wren?
     she's home sick. napping.
     but i could wake her.

no, that's okay.

      your dad's at work still.

i know.

      oh wait! harlow's here.
      let me put you on speakerphone.

mom, you don't have to—

      say "hi harlow!"

umm . . .
hi harlow?

      oh, harlow! it is so cute
      he's looking for you.

my chest aches as i imagine
harlow searching our sad house
for his sad girl.
mom, can you just talk to me?

why? what's wrong?

i curl my body
toward the phone,
a question mark.

can i come home yet?
i want to come home.

mom sighs like
a punctured bicycle tire.
> *no, evie. not until*
> *dr. mantell says you can.*

but you're my mom.
can't you come get me?

> *no, honey. you're sick.*
> *you need to stay there*
> *until you're better.*

my breath hitches.
i promise i'll eat.
as long as i get to come home
i'll eat. please mom.

when she speaks,
it's with the firm voice
she uses when harlow
runs inside with muddy feet.
> *no.*
> *i love you but*
> *the hospital is the best*
> *place for you.*

something inside me
shatters and i want the shards
to cut mom too. i want her
to hurt as much as i do.
if you loved me, you'd never
have left me here.

i hang up the phone,
wrap my arms around
myself, lean against the wall.
create my own illusion,
that someone is
holding me
as i cry.

UNHOOKED

my electrolytes rebalanced,
tammy removes the iv.

no more iv for evie!

the tape rips away
hair and dry, paper skin.
the port is pulled
from my vein,
the needle tickling
as it's extracted—a gory,
burrowing worm.

blood bubbles in the crook
of my arm, runs in a hot, red
rivulet. i reach my index finger
toward the wound, write
my name on my forearm in
swirling, ruby ink.

what are you doing?
that could get infected.

i duck my head, wipe
my bloody finger
on my black leggings.

tammy cleans my arm
with stinging alcohol wipes.
covers the iv site
with a cotton ball and bandage.

"COMMUNITY"

everything is scheduled
here. community meetings
occur monthly. the patients,
on-shift staff, and dr. mantell
gather in the meal room
for a perverse family
meeting, to discuss schedule
changes, menu updates, nurses'
concerns, and patient complaints.

darlene brings in a pink
wooden box, covered in
glitter glue and locked
with a clasp. jayda
leans toward me.

> *this is your first community meeting?*

i nod. she offers
a grim smile.

> *patients put anonymous comments in there.*
> *i call it pandora's box.*

darlene clears her throat,
unfolds a torn strip
of paper. she silently scans

it, rolls her eyes,
then reads aloud
in an uncaring voice.

> *relapsed patients shouldn't be*
> *getting preferential treatment.*
> *they're not sicker,*
> *just weaker.*

the reaction is a traffic
accident. sudden. deadly.
chairs scrape like screeching
brakes as patients
stand, hurl accusations
that land with the crunch
of metal on metal.
the nurses' voices
rise like the wail
of ambulances above.
i sit in the middle,
head spinning,
unable to look away
from the wreckage.

nadia is also seated,
unmoving, jaw tensed
and shoulders inching
toward her ears. jayda
follows my gaze, glares.

did you write this?

nadia sticks her chin out.

so what?

jayda stomps toward nadia,
seizes her shoulders,
holds her down in the chair.
you're disgusting.
this is an illness.
would you say this shit
to a cancer patient?

dr. mantell's stern voice cuts
through the tension.

sit down, jayda.

she doesn't move.
the whole room stops
breathing. jayda pushes nadia
and the chair back two inches.
two nurses bolt over, each
grabs one of jayda's arms,
steer her back
to the chair beside me.

dr. mantell grumbles
in the back of his throat.

you are all sick. sometimes,
i shuffle patients around
to address medication and
behavioral issues because
those take precedence.

the room quiets. all of us stare
at our feet like scolded children.

darlene pulls out another slip of paper.
                    the nurses are intentionally
                    serving room-temperature
                    ensure.

the room explodes
in another argument.

HOW I FEEL

anna listens
too closely—leans
her brown, bobbed
head in, nods as if
my answers to her questions matter.

> *how are you feeling?*
> *how was your week?*
> *how has the unit been?*

fat.
terrible.
hate it.

> *fat isn't a feeling.*

it's how i feel.

> *no, it's not.*
> *delve deeper.*

the hairs on my neck raise
like hackles. who is she
to tell me what i feel?

fine. anxious.

can you explain why?

no.

1500

once dr. mantell is sure
my body will not go
into shock from food—
that i will not literally
die from overeating
like a glutted goldfish—
my calories increase to 1500.

300 extra calories every day.
a slice of strawberry
shortcake at dinner. two
layers of vanilla sponge
separated by strawberry sauce.
icing so sugar-packed
my teeth ache at the sight.
i watch the dessert while
i force dinner down
my throat, as if i expect
it to pull a knife on me.

the gentle weight of a hand
on my shoulder breaks my
staring contest. i face
jayda, a sympathetic smile
on her sylphlike face.

pretend it's another medication
the nurses are giving you.

i swallow my distress.
it's medication. another
substance being forced
into me. this is not my choice.

the fork slides into the soft
porous layers, and i settle a sliver
on my tongue. try not
to taste it. think of dirt
and sugar and vomit,
of yellow globules of fat, as
i chew and gag it in. repeat
until my tongue, teeth, throat
are coated in a sugar film.

jayda applauds.
    brava! brava!
    what a performance!
    how do you feel?

sick and fat.

she pats the top of my head.
    like a good little anorexic, then.

BELLY

the dessert distends
my stomach until
it presses into my
diaphragm, kidneys,
liver. i am a bloated
belly and nothing else.

PANIC ATTACK

i assume the crash position,
       body bent,
       hands on head.
brace for impact.

tammy walks in on me
shaking, gasping, fingernails
dug like fishhooks
into my scalp. she extracts
stiff fingers from my head,
warms my hands between
her rough bony ones.

deep breaths, my girl.
you're safe. you're safe.

the air is gravel
in my lungs. i force it
in and out, the impact
grinding and smoothing
it until it's breathable dust.
my muscles unclench,
my body softening
as much as i will let it.

SHUTTING DOWN

the nurses informed me you had
"paralyzing panic attacks"
twice this past week.

anna examines me
the way children study
ants under a magnifying
glass, burning
the ant alive.

it's fine.
they happen all the time.

it's not fine.
we need to find a way
to control these.

stop feeding me cake.

anna does not even grin.
she considers me,
bites her bottom lip.
her fish tank gurgles.

suppressing all that anxiety,

anger, sadness, fear until you
explode—it's not healthy.

i gaze at my feet. run
my hands along the rough
denim of my jeans.

you're fourteen and already
shutting down. you need
to feel feelings.

i feel things just fine.

are you sure?

i don't respond.
we sit in silent stalemate
until my hour of therapy
is over.

SPACE

during school hours,
away from the unit,
carson, marianne, and i
commiserate over
our least favorite nurses,
medication side effects,
our swollen bellies.

alfred gifts us objects
he finds on walks—pebbles,
pine cones, helicopter seeds
from sycamore trees—and designs
entire science lessons around them.
he recites math equations
as easily as nursery rhymes.
jean dazzles us with
dramatic re-enactments of
historic battles. when she
teaches shakespeare,
she points out all
the sex jokes.

they start each day
with a reminder
that the classroom

is a safe space to express
ourselves. which we do
by swearing. carson sprinkles
assholes and fucks
in his sentences like salt.
marianne reserves swears
for math, muttering

son of a bitch

as she struggles
through algebra. alfred
drops the odd *bastard*
while jean spews ridiculous
elizabethan era insults.
i give the occasional *shit*:
i feel like shit.
the unit is shit.
recovery is shit.

at school, my shoulders
creep away from ears,
limbs loosening the tiniest bit.
i let myself pretend
i am a normal teenager,
not a walking diagnosis.

SUNFLOWER

mom finally visits on day twenty-two
of my captivity. pokes her
head around the privacy
curtain in my room and yells,
> *surprise!*
> *i thought i'd stop by for a visit.*

mom knows i hate surprises.
i also hate how, even though
she tricked me and left
me here for almost a month,
i'm still so happy she's come.
my whole body turns
toward her, a sunflower
following the sun.

SO FUNNY

she takes me off unit—
a privilege i'm only allowed
with adult supervision—
to the cafeteria, where
she orders a coffee.
>*you're looking so healthy, evie.*

translation:
>you've gained weight.

how's harlow?

>*harlow stopped eating*
>*much after you left.*
>*the vet said it's depression.*

my vision flashes
snow white as
a jolt of panic
charges through me.
is he okay?

>*yes, he's fine. he's eating again.*
>*but it's so funny!*

my daughter's depressed and not eating
and now my dog is too.

how do i respond to that?
yes mom. hilarious.

OUTBURST

everything's normal at home.
wren's always off with friends.
your dad and i keep busy
with work.

her breath hitches. i notice
the dark circles
beneath her eyes.
she's skinnier.
she's lost weight.
i seethe. how dare
she lose weight
when i'm being forced
to gain it.

mom gulps her coffee
without blowing on it first.
for her, hot drinks are to be
finished, not savored.

your hospitalization has been hard on me.
i haven't slept much. luckily, my coworkers
have been supportive since i explained.

my blood turns to cement

my heart cannot churn.
explained?
you told them?

      yes, i needed to talk to someone.

why would you tell anyone?
my voice is fire alarm shrill.
the people beside us
relocate. loud
whispers float from
the table of men
in blue scrubs.

      you're being hysterical.
      you're not the only one
      going through this, evie.

funny, i haven't seen
you in the line for
morning weigh-in.

SHAME

she takes me back
to the unit without
saying another word.

i am drowning in shame
about my outburst.
i should apologize.

but i won't.

i doubt mom feels shame
about anything. except
having me for a daughter.

1800

my weight plateaus
and my calories rise
to 1800 a day.
my stomach knots
around a burning ball
of half-digested food.
the flames of gastric juices
flicker up my throat.
i breathe fire, fantasize
i am a dragon girl
setting the unit alight,
scorching it until it's
nothing but a smoldering,
black carcass.

OCTOBER

WHEN GRAVITY WAS
WELCOME

october arrives in a blaze
of yellow, orange, and red that
i view from the hospital window.

wren and i used to rake
leaves into piles. once
they were heaped
as high as our heads,
we would count down:
three, two, one . . .
launch ourselves,
heedless of sharp
sticks, into the mounds.

gravity was welcome
then, the crunch of leaves
under my body relished.
i'd reach out my limbs,
wave them back and forth,
imprint angels
in the itchy leaves.
            the larger the better.

i'd walk around the house
perfumed in the wet scent
of decay, scraps of brown,
yellow, and orange shedding
from my body like skin.

TINY FANTASY

jayda flops across
my bed. each
of her individual
ribs digs into my feet.
if i ran my instep up
her torso, i could play
her like a xylophone.

she speaks with a terrible
british accent.
>   *i'm bored. would you care to*
>   *take a turn about the room?*
then in her normal voice.
>   *please say yes. i'm going*
>   *stir-crazy. you're the only*
>   *other patient who isn't*
>   *blacking out on anti-anxieties*
>   *or too irritating to handle.*

i wiggle
my toes, tickling her
warm belly.
i'll need my legs to walk.

she stands, squares

her shoulders, puffs
out her chest,
and offers me her arm.
   m'lady?

i accept with a curtsy,
wrap my arm through
hers, our bony elbows
knocking against each other.
i pretend i'm tall, slim,
perfect keira knightley.
m'lord.

we pace in circles
around the unit, ignore
the nurses' discreet
observance, speak
in fake accents. when
we pass patients sleeping
in the hallway chairs,
jayda says,
   my, what vibrant wildlife
   this city offers.

we manage nine laps
before darlene yells
at us to stop. her voice
is a sharp tack bursting
our tiny fantasy.

she threatens to feed us extra
calories if our obsessive exercise
continues. jayda drops
the accent, whispers,
          temperamental twat.

RELIEF

in group, tammy
discusses the dangers
of social media
for people like us—
the sick and
starved, always
searching for better
ways to be both.

if you're going to heal,
you need a supportive
environment—
on and offline. so today
we're scrubbing our
social media.

she plunks a plastic
bin full of our phones
in the center of the room.
we flock like pigeons pecking
up birdseed, arms and elbows
as angular as wings.

cradling my phone
in the palm of my hand
feels like scratching a stubborn
itch on the sole of my foot.

AT LEAST

it does until
tammy makes us
open apps, unfollow
accounts, delete
bookmarks, obliterate
anything that mentions
      diets
      cleanses
      exercise
      body size.
then it feels like
i'm plucking eyelashes
one by one.

especially when i give
in to temptation and check
the cherry-red notifications
on instagram. discover
messages from darcy
but also questions
from classmates
i've never spoken to:

            why aren't you at school?
        yo, is it true ur pregnant?
did you transfer?

i heard you died.

        u rlly in the crazy hospital?

i delete everyone
except darcy.
set my account
to private. return
my phone to tammy's
bin before she even
asks for it back.

MOTHER AND DAUGHTER

since her disastrous visit
i refuse to call mom,
hold tight to this last
tiny piece of control.
she can only contact me
by calling the decrepit
patient phone. the ringer is
a piercing trill, an alarm
that wakes patients from
their naps.

neither of us brings up
the fight—avoidance is
too deeply rooted in our genes.
she asks me how i am,
i lie and say i'm fine.
we pretend to be
a good mother, a good
daughter, though neither
of us knows which role
the other is playing.

THIRTY DAYS

on day thirty of captivity
i knock on dr. mantell's door.
he waves me in without
looking up from the chart
he's scribbling on, bent so
far over that his nose skims
the surface.

dr. mantell, i—

he raises his index finger
toward me, his eyes
still fixed on the paper. he finishes
with a flourish of his pen,
rolls his neck left and right.

what do you need?

i grip my hands in fists
to hide their trembling.
i've been here one month.

so you have.

thirty days.

yes.

you said you'd consider
letting me leave
after that time.

he steeples his fingers
together. arches an eyebrow.
                    did i?

how does he not remember?
yes.

                do you really think
                you're healthy enough to leave?

though his voice lilts
upward, it does not feel
like he's asking a question.
i do not reply.

dr. mantell retrieves my chart
from the nurses' desk.
cracks the spine of the
bulky binder and flips
through pages.

                you're still well below
                your goal weight.

the nurses have noted
numerous compulsive
behaviors, and anna's session
notes do not indicate a positive
shift in thought patterns.

but i've eaten all
my meals. i promise
i'll continue eating
at home.
i flinch at how whiny
my voice is. i sound like
a spoiled child.

dr. mantell rustles through
more pages. taps his fingers
on the table. heat flutters
at the base of my neck
in time with the tapping.

you're not on a sustainable
calorie level yet. actually . . .
i'm going to bump you up.

the heat sears
through the rest
of my body.
i'm being cooked
from the inside out.

wait. what?

                    we'll increase your calories
                    to 2100, starting today.

my jaw quivers.
you just put me at 1800.

                    if you can't eat 2100 calories
                    why do you think you can leave?

i bite my cheeks, clench
my fists until my
fingernails nip my palms
and my skin throbs.
how much longer will
i be here?

                    that depends entirely on you.

2100

my stomach marches itself
into knots, jams picket signs
deep into my intestines.

i cannot finish a meal
without gagging. the nurses
substitute my remaining
solid food with ensure
so i don't choke.

darlene shakes her head
when my dry heaving starts.

keep this up and we'll
give you a feeding tube.

FEEDING TUBE

it sounds like something
from a dystopian sci-fi film.
none of the other patients
are hooked to hoses
inflating them.

MENTORSHIP

darlene's full of shit.
she doesn't have the power
to give you a tube.

jayda and i turn
right, on our second
clockwise lap
around the unit.

mantell is in charge
of all the big decisions.
the nurses are just his cronies.

she teaches me other lessons:

never ask the younger nurses
for an ensure replacement.
they always overestimate calories.

it's easy to sneak in jumping
jacks, squats, or push-ups
at night because the nurses
only check in hourly.

lower your calories
by ordering chicken, oreos,
cornflakes, or pudding—
each item is thirty calories less
than the menu states.

> it's okay to push back
> against the unit's rules
> a bit. little cheats don't
> matter in the long run.

LITTLE CHEATS

the hard slap
of water on tile
covers my panting:
one hundred squats,
one hundred crunches,
fifty push-ups.

by the time i'm done
the mirror is fogged
and the shower runs
cool. i slump, my pulse
flitting hummingbird
fast from exertion and
the small thrill of getting
away with something.

little cheats are okay.

i lather my head with
shampoo, rinse away
sweat and remorse.

TEENS ONLY

sunday afternoon, i follow
laughter—loud and rare—
to the patient lounge,
find carson and marianne
giggling at a cartoon playing
on the old tv.

teens only!
carson shouts.

marianne rolls her eyes.
if you look away
for, like, one second
you'll see evie is *a teen.*

carson turns to me then
and smiles.
teen evie!
have a seat.

i choose one of
the recliners between
him and marianne,
tuck my body up
as small as it will go.

carson offers me a can
of diet orange soda
but i shake my head.
thank you. but i can't.
my stomach—

he interjects.

> *say no more.*
> *growing pains.*
> *i get it.*

what are you watching?
the show is some
poorly drawn, raunchy
adult cartoon. the kind
mom never lets
wren and me put on.

marianne fiddles with
one of her dark braids.

> *it's not, like,*
> *high art or anything*
> *but it helps drown out*
> *all of this.*

she gestures at
the walls boxing us in.

carson laughs.

> *dude, this is a stoner show.*

it's the definition of "high art."

i sit for an hour before
i get so antsy i need
to leave. as i exit,
carson calls after me.

teen club meets every sunday.
see you next week!

BACK DOWN

i'm sneaking in calf raises,
listening for the rumble
of the breakfast cart, when
the bathroom door slams open
and candace's high voice says,
                    evie. we need to talk.

i open the curtains and find
candace wearing nothing
but a towel, red hair resting
on freckled shoulders, eyes
overflowing with disdain.

hey.

                    hey.
                    look. i know you like
                    "long showers," but this is
                    the third morning in a row
                    i've had cold water.

my face goes hot.
sorry. i'll be more
careful from now on.

maybe save your "showers"
for when i'm not around, okay?
i'm close to getting out
and don't need you bringing me
back down to your level.

her words are a hard
slap to my face.

she marches to her bed,
shuts her curtain, leaves me
stunned and scratching
the scabs on my scalp.

NEGOTIATIONS

> *your mom has requested*
> *an evening pass for you*
> *this saturday.*

anna's announcement
sends a nauseous ripple
of surprise through my stomach.
she didn't mention anything.

> *she contacted dr. mantell.*

i snort.
of course she did.

> *it would be for an evening.*
> *you'd have dinner at home*
> *and be back for snack.*
> *the doctor asked me if i think*
> *you're ready for that.*

i'm ready.

> *i'm not so sure.*

i shake my head

in frustration.
why?

> *you've been here a month but*
> *you still avoid talking about your*
> *family. i don't think it's a healthy*
> *environment for you right now.*

i love my family.
they love me.

> *i don't doubt that, but family*
> *is never that simple.*

please, anna.

she picks at a loose
thread on her skirt.
i scratch at a sore on
the nape of my neck.

> *okay. but we have a full*
> *debrief next session*
> *and we talk about*
> *your family. no avoidance.*
> *deal?*

yes, anything. deal.

SUMMER VACATION,
ONE YEAR AGO

i remember driving
to the mountains, sitting
in the back of the car
legs curled beneath me,
the seat belt cutting red lines
into my neck. wren watched
movies on our mom's ipad,
the cartoon voices floating
like helium through the air.
mom reaching for my dad's hand,
rested on the gear shift.
he turned his palm up,
interlaced his fingers in hers,
gave a small squeeze.

we stopped for a picnic
lunch of ham sandwiches,
laughed at a pair of chipmunks
fighting over scraps.

that's what this pass
will be like too.
my parents will remember

how good things are
with me around. they'll
remember how much they
love me and they won't
send me back.

PASS DAY

i stare at the clock,
pace, pick my scalp,
play through multiple
scenarios for the evening
in my head.
excitement and nerves
bubble in my stomach
like latte foam.

jayda joins me in the hallway,
where i have a clear view
of the unit's exit.

>   *nervous?*

a bit. more excited,
you know?

>   *yeah. that's how i feel*
>   *when i get passes with my husband.*

you have a husband?

she nods, a mournful
glint in her eyes.

just some advice:
this might not go the way
you imagine. the world keeps moving
while you're in here.

i purse my lips, begin
to ask what she means,
when the staccato clack
of expensive shoes
announces mom's arrival.

ON LOAN

mom signs me out
like i'm a library book.

a nurse outlines
the terms of my loan:
> *you cannot take her on stairs.*
> *no bathrooms for an hour after eating.*
> *bring her back before eight p.m.*

i walk out
the double doors,
give the unit a boastful
backward glance.

THE PATIENT

we are rushing down
the highway when mom asks,
*who was that woman
you were speaking to?*

the nurse?

*no.
the patient.*

it takes too long
for me to realize
she means jayda.
the nurses call us all
girls, never women.

*that's jayda.
she's sort of like
a friend.*

mom sucks in
her lips until her mouth
is a pencil-thin line.
how old is she?

i don't know.
older than me,
like everyone there,
i reply, leaning into
the window and ending
the conversation.

SUMMER VACATION,
ONE YEAR AGO
THE TRUTH

my memories of family
vacation weren't exactly accurate.
i remember now that the sandwiches
were slathered in mayo,
layered with creamy havarti
and slices of ham so thick
veins of fat ran through them.

i only pretended to eat,
took bite after bite but
never swallowed. chewed
until the sandwich turned
to glue and my jaw ached.
tongued the food into
the pockets of my cheeks.

i carried my family's garbage
to the bin. leaned in.
the stench of rotting fruit,
dog shit, and other trash
made my eyes water.
i choked out the pulpy mess
of non-digested food,

slammed down the lid, and
felt a mix of shame,
pride, disgust, elation.

i returned, sure my parents
would know what
i'd done, would smell
the reek of wastefulness
on me. but my mother
jumped in surprise.

> *evie! no one even noticed*
> *you had left!*

THE PASS

dad is called into work
to deal with an issue
that cannot wait.

wren stumbles over words
like a toddler just learning
to speak. she says little.

mom says too much
about the color in
my cheeks, how much
healthier i look.

only harlow acts right.
he whines and jumps
when i arrive, fetches
his favorite toy bat,
and barks until i
throw it. he does not
let me out of his sight.

TASTE NOTHING

mom serves creamy,
fatty spaghetti carbonara
that stinks of grease.
she supervises me
like a suspicious schoolmarm
as i struggle to swallow,
gives me a second serving
when i finish the first.
this is more calories
than the unit gives me.

she explodes.
> *why is food always a fight with you?*
> *you're supposed to be getting better.*

there are tears in her eyes.
wren looks away—
embarrassed by her sick
sister destroying the family
because she won't eat.

i force down the spaghetti,
tasting nothing but
> sawdust.

DERMATILLOMANIA

i excuse myself
from the table
the moment i'm finished.

> *you're not allowed*
> *alone after meals,*
mom reminds me.
as if i could forget.
it's just my room.
you can literally hear
through the ceiling
if i try sneaking
to the bathroom.

she's too exhausted
with me to fight.
> *your door stays open.*

i climb the mountain
of stairs to my room,
harlow trailing
and whimpering behind.

i am fat. i am a
failure. i am a difficult

child. i am breaking
my family apart.

my limbs are heavy
and large. moving them
is like swimming
through a pool
of maple syrup.

my chest heaves
with the exertion of
holding back tears.

i reach both hands
up to my head and
scratch and scratch and scratch
while harlow whines and whines.
but i do not stop.
i rake nails across scalp
until a sharp, burning pain
makes me hiss.

i whip my hands
in front of my face.
wedged under my right
fingernails is a knot
of hair, skin, blood.
i yank it out, drop it.
harlow skulks toward

the tangle, sniffs.

harlow, leave it!

i grab two handfuls
of tissues from a box
beside my bed—press one
to my bleeding scalp,
pick up the wet ball
of hair with the other.
when the bleeding stops,
i bury all evidence
in my dresser, under
piles of old, stained underwear.

BACK TO THE SHITHOLE

the next morning,
my pillowcase is covered
in light brown stains.
i trace my new sore—
a hard crust with liquid
seeping through the cracks.
relief and pain
wash through me
as i pick open the scab.
it is the size of a nickel,
dark and dry
as a strip of beef jerky.

it stands out against
my pale hand, could be
mistaken for a trespassing
beetle. i drop it in the trash.
with a flip, the pillow
becomes clean. unspoiled.
in the shower, i rub shampoo
into the reopened wound,
the welcoming sting
deserved.

CAMARADERIE

i sit across the lounge
from carson and marianne,
curled in on myself
like an armadillo,
my quietness a loud
announcement of yesterday's
disaster.

as the end credits roll,
marianne wrings her hands,
her dark knuckles dry
and cracked, says,

> *on my first pass home, i snuck*
> *six diet pills from my stash.*
> *they irritated my stomach*
> *so much, i puked. my parents*
> *brought me right back and*
> *i wasn't allowed off-unit*
> *for a month.*

she looks at carson,
who laughs.

> *you think that's bad?*
> *my first pass was in august.*
> *it was so fucking hot but i still*

wore *fleece sweats and a hoodie.*
passed out from heat exhaustion
and woke up to paramedics
loading me into an ambulance.

marianne snorts.

> *the first visit home*
> *is a test that no one passes.*

we all turn back
to the tv. sit with our silences
the rest of the afternoon.

GOOD AT ALL

instead of learning about
invasive species, i sit,
face in my textbook,
replaying my catastrophic
pass. i should have begged
dad to stay. i shouldn't
have complained about
calories. i should have
been better. i push
on my sore until
my toes curl
with the burn.

there's a rustling
beside me, the earthy
smell of soil. alfred
folds into a short
plastic chair. his knees
reach his armpits
and his pants creep
up his legs, revealing
shins as hairy as
the rest of him.

everything okay?

sorry. i'm having
trouble concentrating.

don't apologize.
let's go through
the lesson together.

he reads aloud from
my textbook, his voice
as soft as a spring breeze.
i focus on his words,
quiet my mind, stop
pushing on my wound.

when class is done,
alfred gives me a sticker—
a rainbow that says
"good job" even though
i did nothing. it's stupid
and for kids. still, it's nice
to have someone think
i'm any good at all.
i stick it to the back
of my hand, wear it until
it falls off later that night.

GAINING

my weight continues
to crawl upward.
i can barely wrap
my thumb and middle
finger around my bicep.

pockets of fat bud
from my chest,
push my nipples out,
forcing me to wear
bras again. the band digs
into my ribs, imprints
my skin in
punishing pink pits.

i sit through class
no longer squirming in
discomfort. i ask jean
if she replaced the chairs.

they're the same as always.

they don't hurt anymore.

her eyes and mouth
soften with sympathy.
>   *that's because you're no longer*
>   *sitting directly on bone.*

WHAT I WANT

how was your pass?

i reach for the inflamed
scab on my scalp,
drop my hand under
anna's scrutinizing gaze.
okay, i think.

> *remember, talking about your family*
> *was a condition of it.*

i swallow the lump
of anxiety crawling
up my throat.
it could have been better.

> *better how?*

i thought, maybe,
things would be different.

> *you wanted to be treated differently*
> *because you're sick?*

the hairs on my neck

172

prickle and rise.
no. i don't know.
i expected things to be
normal but better.

        and what would that look like?

i don't know.

        you must know
        if it's what you expected.

my stomach is a sea
of bubbling, booming
digestive juices.
i scratch a new section
on my head.
i don't want to complain
about my family. nothing
is wrong with them.

anna's eyes are full
of too much pity.
i shift my gaze
to the fish whirling
in her tank.
        do you want to feed them?

what?

the fish.
do you want to feed them?

i nod my head.
she opens a cylindrical
container next
to the tank. tiny pink flakes
similar to the skin
i scrape from my scalp
fill it to the brim.

        grab a pinch
        and sprinkle it over
        the surface.

the fishy smell of
the food makes me
seasick, but i follow
anna's instructions.
the fish flock
to the surface,
their gaping mouths
inhaling the food.
the bottom feeder waits
for the leftovers to fall
to the rocks below, sucks
them up like a vacuum.

        they're relaxing to watch,
        aren't they?

yeah.

anna is silent
for a few moments.
> *evie, i know you love your*
> *family. i'm not trying to*
> *change that. i'm trying*
> *to figure out how best*
> *to help you heal.*

i take a shallow breath.

> *can you answer one*
> *question for me?*

i do not look away
from the fish tank
when i reply.
maybe.

> *what do you want from your family?*

the good girl in me
needs to please anna.
the rippling water
reminds me of dad
always disappearing
to work. of wren floating
among her circle of friends.

of mom, evasive, never still.
of me, caught in the tide
of my family's
constant leaving.

i pretend i'm in the
fish tank, the room around
me morphed by
the refraction of water.

i want them to notice me
when i'm not sick and dying.

RED-HANDED

when I return to my room
jayda is cross-legged
on my bed, my pillow
resting in her lap
stained side up.
the corners of her mouth
quirk up, an impish grin.
a fist grips my gut, juices
it like a lemon.

her spider-long legs unfurl.
she motions for me
to follow her to the bathroom,
pillowcase trailing.

the door shuts
conspiratorially
behind us.
> *cold water and soap*
> *works best for bloodstains.*

the fabric shushes
like sandpaper as she
scrubs it against itself,

her knuckles knocking
against each other.
the stains bubble,
disappear down the drain
in a stream of brown.

THE WEIRDEST SCHOOL

with jean's permission,
i check my now-gutted
instagram, find a new message
from darcy. i steel myself
for more questions, more
of my patented avoidance.

instead, i find
she's written

to cheer u up

and sent along
a video of a howling
dalmatian, paws banging
on a piano. the full volume
blast reverberates through
the classroom. everyone
jumps. i fumble
for the speakers.

jean's laughter overpowers
the howling. she sings
in perfect harmony.
alfred applauds,
his faux italian accent
butchering,

brava! bella! bravissima!

jean clasps his hands.
    come, amore mio.
    dance with me!
and the two of them
tango, quite terribly,
up and down the room
as the video loops.

carson doubles over
laughing and clapping.
    this is the weirdest fucking school.
    i love it.

WARNINGS

alone in the patient
lounge, sprawled
across a recliner,
i page through an old
people magazine in search
of exercise and weight
loss tips when another
patient, kristy, finds me.
she settles her soft curves
in the seat to my right.

                    can we talk?

my spine stiffens. all
i know about kristy
is that she's jayda's
bulimic roommate.

about what?

                    jayda.

she crosses her legs,
leans forward, her shirt
gaping to reveal fistfuls

of cleavage. jayda once
confessed she was scared
she'd look like kristy
when she reached
her goal weight.

*you need to be careful
with her. she's sick.
really sick. she has
a nasty habit of dragging
people down with her.*

i glare.
a secret jayda
told me flies out
of my mouth:
*this coming from the girl
who keeps bags of vomit
in her closet.*

kristy recoils, her face
flushing a deep shade
of red, as though struck.

*who do you think
i learned that from?*

her lips curl with disdain.
she rockets herself

out of the chair, rushes
from the room. i riffle,
ashamed, through glossy
magazine pages, tear out
a page about a juice cleanse
to try when i'm home.

DISCHARGED

candace hauls two
suitcases and her backpack
to the nurses' desk and signs
her discharge papers.
she hugs tammy, darlene,
and the other nurses, pulls
away glassy-eyed and smiling.

her parents each clutch
a suitcase and wrap
an arm around her shoulders.
they walk out the doors
looking like a three-
headed beast.

darlene catches me
peeking from behind
my bedroom door frame.

> *enjoy the private room*
> *while you can. you'll have*
> *a new roommate*
> *within the week.*

i retreat inside,
lie on candace's unwashed

bedsheets, imagining discharge
is contagious, trying to
soak it up through
my pallid skin.

"HEALTHY"

darlene fiddles with
the electronic scale.
the peeps sound
like a distressed r2-d2.
my teeth grind
tighter with each beep.

remove your hoodie, shoes,
and jeans.

the wobbly platform seeps
cold into my feet.
my bare legs pucker
with goose bumps.
my eyes squeeze shut,
unwilling to see
my increased failure.

good job. you're getting
much healthier.

healthier means fatter,
i'm fatter. i sneak a glance.
only ten pounds away
from my goal weight.

ANOREXIC DEFINITIONS

food—
    a substance that leads
    to weight gain.
    to be avoided.

trigger—
    fatty food, sugary food,
    models, instagram, fat bodies,
    slim bodies, medium bodies,
    any body, the number on the scale,
    the number of steps taken,
    the number on a food label,
    the number on my clothes.

healthy—
    fat.

disciplined
    not eating.

beautiful—
    thin.

enough—
    what i'll never be.

HALLOWEEN

instead of dressing up with
darcy, i'm surrounded
by the skeletons and ghouls
of the other patients.

the dietitian delivers
a box of mini halloween
chocolates to the meal
room. tells us we can
substitute our dessert
for candy.

yeah right.

chocolate sticks to
the edges of teeth, right
along the gums where
tartar builds. i have no
desire to tongue, slurp,
and suck chocolate from
my teeth, to have my skin
bubble with chocolate
pimples and chocolate
cellulite. turn into

a chocolate-covered
failure.

NOVEMBER

FIELD TRIP

on one of the last
warm days of fall,
alfred and jean take us
to the river valley.
we wander tree-lined
trails. alfred teaches
us the latin names for
sparrow, magpie, and crow.
jean warbles a gentle
aria that ripples with
the water. carson, marianne,
and i welcome the heat
of sunlight on our faces
after too many days
of cool fluorescent lights.

2400

mantell ups me
again. and it's
hell. again.

my temperature regulation
goes berserk. i am either
freezing from a ghost-cold
draft or menopausal, stripping
off layers and praying
that my pools of sweat
are deep enough to drown in.

my thighs chafe against
each other, my butt cheeks
clap when i walk.
my breasts engorge.
the soft tissue
sways as i reach my fork
across my tray and scoop
mashed potatoes into my mouth.

NEW ROOMMATE

she shows up within
a week, like darlene warned.
dropped off by her husband
and two young sons.
olena, my new roommate, is
a dried-out cinnamon stick,
brittle enough to snap.

the nurses give her
a feeding tube, a thick
white worm that tunnels
up her nose, down
into her stomach.
it is the only way
she can eat with her
arfid—avoidant restrictive
food intake disorder.
anything harder than
a soft, ripe banana
makes her fear she will
choke and die.

she phones her family
every night at nine p.m.
—her sons' bedtime.

her loud, wet sobs
become the soundtrack
of my sleep.

BRANDISH

within days, another girl,
nadia, gets a feeding tube
too. she makes a point
of wearing her hair back
in a ponytail, draws
attention to the tube
like a recently engaged woman
flashing her new ring.

DISFIGURED

evie, you're bleeding!
anna jumps from her chair
and grabs my right hand.
my fingertips are damp. blood
has congealed beneath my nails,
a sticky red jelly.
i didn't even notice
i was scratching.

wait here, i'll be right back.

the bubble of the fish tank
barely masks her frantic
exchange with the nurses.
drawers and cabinets
slam open and shut.

she returns carrying
a bottle of rubbing alcohol
and cotton pads.
where's the wound?

reluctantly, i part the hair
around my sore.
the bottle gurgles

its liquid loose. anna
leans so close, her breath
tickles my ear.

this may sting.

cold cotton dabs at
my head. it burns.
i do not flinch.
it's a familiar pain.

there's a rustle as anna
tosses out the bloodied
pads. then her warm fingers
pick through my hair
like a mother chimp
grooming her baby.
she discovers the red pits
carved into my head.

oh, evie.

shame bursts through
the dam of my heart,
gushes until my body
is heavy with it.
tears run haphazard
down my face,
my shoulders shudder

with violent sobs.

i am disgusting.
i am damaged.
i am disfigured.

the warmth of anna's hands
seeps into my scalp.
her gentle fingers smooth
the mess of my hair.

GROUNDING

anna jumps into
action like some
therapeutic superhero.

evie, we're going to go through
a grounding exercise to get you
out of your panic.
focus on five things you can see.

my red-stained nails.
anna leaning over me.
the fish, swimming.
the tank's multicolored rocks.
my gray-socked feet.

what are four things you can touch?

my tacky, bloody fingers.
anna's warm brown hands.
the cool vinyl of the chair.
the hard knob of my left knee.

what are three things you hear?

my haggard breath.
babbling tank water.
air rattling through a vent.

two things you smell?

sharp rubbing alcohol.
anna's eucalyptus hand lotion.

one thing you can taste?

the faint hint of bile
retreating down my throat.

you're safe, evie.
you're safe.

CURBING IMPULSES

anna digs nail clippers
out of her purse,
watches me cut my nails
flush to my fingertips.

> *you'll keep them short*
> *until you stop scratching.*

she creaks open
a cupboard, pulls out
a box of wax crayons.

> *to help you with your*
> *picking urge.*

i pinch the box's smooth
cardboard corners.

> *the next time difficult*
> *emotions come up*
> *destroy a crayon instead*
> *of yourself. remind yourself*
> *that your emotions are valid.*
> *you're allowed to feel.*

*i know. i just wish
i felt more
than hurt.*

SHREDDED

the patient phone's harsh
trill reverberates through
the unit for a minute straight.
it stops, replaced by carson's
low bellow.

> *evie, it's for you!*

i trudge to the phone
alcove, pick up the
dangling receiver.
hello?

mom's voice answers.

> *evie, is that you?*

yeah.

> *hi honey! how are you?*

her tone is overly
cheerful. she must not have
been told about the pockmarked
state of my scalp.
i'm okay.
how are you?

things are great here!
have you talked to wren?
she was cast as the lead
in the school play.
the lead! that girl definitely
takes after me.

which i interpret as:
"thank god i can be proud
of one of my daughters."

my head tingles, fingers
twitch with the urge
to scratch. instead,
i skin the wrapper off
a coffee-brown crayon.
insert practiced
one-word responses.
oh.
neat.
wow.
uh-huh.

i've arranged another pass
for next week.
that will be fun, right?

the wrapper shredded,
i move on to the crayon's wax.

it comes up in curlicues, colors
my nails and fingertips
a rich brown.
yeah. so fun.

  i'll see you next saturday.
  i miss you, love you.

still on autopilot,
I respond,
yep.

    what?

i mean, you too.
see you later.

we hang up.
i smear the mess
of mangled crayon
at my feet
into the floor.

MESSY

when i return to my room,
olena eyes my stained fingers.

          what's that?

she asks, her polish accent
lending the question
the cadence of a song.

a side effect of talking
with my mom.

i retreat to the bathroom,
wash tacky wax from my
fingertips. when i'm done,
i sit in the window well,
watch the parking lot below.

through the curtain
separating our beds,
i hear olena clear her throat.

          you know, it's not easy.
          being a mom.

my heart quickens.
candace and i rarely
talked to each other.

we pretended thin curtains
provided real privacy,
that we couldn't hear
each other through
threadbare walls.

i take a moment to respond.
it's not easy being a daughter.

olena chuckles.
> *that's true. what i mean though*
> *is mothers do the best*
> *we can and sometimes—*

her voice cracks
and i hear sniffles.
> *sorry. i know it's not my place*
> *to say this. but moms are human*
> *and sometimes we mess up.*

how do i explain
that i think *i* am
my mom's mess-up?

A FAVOR

the clock slowly counts
down the minutes until supper,
the second hand lurching
like a clumsy toddler
taking its first steps.
i've been lying upside down,
head hung off the edge
of the bed since 4:17 p.m.

jayda's moon-white face
eclipses the ticking clock.

what're you doing?

with a startled squeak
i flip right-side up. the room
spins, flashing lights cloud
my vision as blood rushes
from my head. it takes three
deep breaths for the world
to return to normal.

can you do me a favor?

yeah, what?

she pulls a bottle of ibuprofen

from the folds of her
enormous knit sweater.

could you hide these for me?
my husband's picking me up
for my pass soon. the nurses
search my room when i'm gone
and i don't want them finding
these and getting the wrong idea.

my brows knit together.
i thought all our pills
were kept in the med room.

prescription meds.
you can buy these over the counter.

so, you're allowed
to have them?

totally.

then why hide them?

jayda's laugh is mean.
the nurses can be stupid
strict because some patients
abuse medication. i need
these for bad tension headaches.

i reach a hand
to scratch my scalp,
but my nails
are too short.
where'd you get them?

she grins, flashes her
wrist, a white band.
>   *upgraded from the orange*
>   *band this morning.*
>   *stopped by a pharmacy*
>   *on my walk. what do you say,*
>   *can you hide them for me?*

the clock ticks and ticks
and ticks and ticks and
it almost sounds like
it's saying:
>   *e-vie don't.*
>   *e-vie don't.*

yeah, sure.

>   *thanks! i owe you.*

she hands me the rattling
bottle. i stick it in a bunched-up
pair of socks in my closet.
jayda squeezes my shoulder,
leaves me with the
disapproving clock.

SATURDAY SNOW

i wake to a quieter, calmer
world. a dusting of snow,
light as baby powder,
coats the courtyard outside.
i press my forehead against
the cool glass of the window,
smudge it with my skin's
morning oil, breathe in the
stillness of snow-covered streets.

BUSTED

not thinking,
i pick up
my bunched socks.
the bottle flies out,
falls to the floor,
jangles and rolls out
the door, toward
the nurses' desk,
clatters to a stop
against the toe
of darlene's
sensible shoes.

COVER

i'm slumped in the seat
across from dr. mantell
and his stupid nameplate
again. the ibuprofen bottle
stands at attention
in the no-man's-land of desk
between me and him.

why do you have these?

a good girl, an abiding
girl, would tell him, but
if i snitch on jayda
they'll take away her
hard-earned privileges.
she'll lose her daily
walks, her passes home.
they're mine.

i don't believe you.

when he stares at me
with his sharp gray eyes
i do not look away.
my palms sit moist in my lap,

214

heat burns my cheeks.
my voice squeaks as
i repeat,
they are mine.

mantell breaks first,
looks at my chart
and scratches illegible code.
for several minutes,
graphite scraping paper
and the blood pounding in
my ears are the only sounds.

he stretches his neck,
releases a drawn-out sigh.
                    you can go.
                    the pills stay with me.

shock cracks me
like a knuckle
across the jaw.
that's it?

                    that's it.

but i broke the rules.

he steeples his fingers
and, like a movie villain,

gazes over them at me.

i highly doubt that,
given you can't leave the unit.

his words rattle me
like a bottle of ibuprofen.
my mouth goes dry.

let's hope your actions have no
future consequences.

my knees pop as i stand,
creak while i walk
out the office door.

NEXT TIME

how i want my
conversation with jayda
to go:

you lied to me
about the meds.
they're not allowed.
you made me break
the rules.

   you're right.
   i'm so sorry.
   i don't know what
   i was thinking.
   can you ever forgive me?

if you promise to never
use me again.

how it really goes:

   thanks for covering
   for my fat ass
   with mantell.

you told me
the meds were
allowed.

> *god, they should be,*
> *right? everyone here*
> *is so fucking controlling.*

they confiscated
the bottle.

> *don't worry.*
> *i'll hide it better*
> *next time.*

CHARTING

anna and i create a chart
of the emotions
i don't let myself
feel:
>sadness

>anxiety

>anger

>fear

and anna helps me
brainstorm healthy
responses to them:
>cry

>breathe

>go for a walk

>acknowledge the feeling

she folds the lined
loose leaf into quarters,
the creases sharp enough to cut.

>*if you feel any of these*
>*on your pass, find a*
>*space to be alone and*
>*consult this chart.*

i pluck it from her outstretched
hand, tuck it in the back
pocket of my jeans, beside three
mangled crayons. tears
tingle at the backs
of my eyes, the roof
of my mouth starts to quiver.
i inhale a heavy
gulp of air.
i'm scared i'll mess this up.
again.

the corners of anna's
mouth curl up.

> *i understand. but i know*
> *you're tough enough*
> *to handle this.*

SPOTTED

pre-pass anxiety pulsates
in my fingers, urges me
to pick at anything—
sweater cuffs, corners
of papers, the loose thread
on my jeans.

i destroy six
different crayons:
scarlet,
apricot,
magenta,
carnation pink,
red orange,
violet red.
scrape up curls
of wax that gum
up my fingernails.

in class, jean reads
through *macbeth*
with carson. when she
recites the lines
     "out, damned spot.
     out i say,"

carson glances at my
red-dyed fingers.
i stare him dead
in the eye and pretend
to wash my hands.
he guffaws and jean
suppresses a small smile.

when a nurse arrives
to escort us back
to the unit, jean tucks
a new crayon box
into my stained hands.

PREPARATIONS

i dress in pants that rest
loosely on my hipbones,
smooth brown belt
holding them up,
my blackest t-shirt,
the men's forest-green
hoodie that hangs halfway
to my knees. my emotion chart
tucked in my back pocket
alongside wisteria, plum,
and vivid violet crayons
—three shades of purple
to pick apart.

armored and armed,
i stand watch by the doors,
shifting from foot to foot.
mom marches in ten minutes late,
her face one giant grin.

ready to go?

ready.

HOME AGAIN

the front door opens to
a spotless entry,
shoes and coats hidden neatly away.

whimpers and scratches
rebound from the back
of the house. a door scrapes
open, nails skitter across
laminate floor, my dad shouts,
                    go get her!
and harlow rounds the corner,
snowballs flying from his
mop of black fur, puddles
dripping from his paws.
he barrels into my knees
and i crumple, laughing,
into a pile on the floor.
harlow leaps all over me,
squishes my lungs, crushes
my shoulders, steps on
my face. soon, i'm as
snow-soaked as he is.

mom gasps, yanks harlow
off long enough for me

to stand, remove my coat.

      peter, look at this mess!

dad slinks over,
a sheepish smile on his face.

                sorry. i thought it would
                be funny.

harlow escapes mom's grasp,
jumps up and places
his paws on either side
of my torso, like a hug.
i bury my face
in his fur, let his wet-dog
scent overpower the metallic
odor of my anxiety.

THE SECOND PASS

dad stays home,
turns his phone to silent
and leaves it on the counter.
his usual suit and tie replaced
with a wool sweater
and timeworn jeans.

wren chatters in nonstop
run-on sentences about
the school play, performs
half-choreographed dances.
when she cartwheels,
her yellow shirt bunches
at her waist, displaying
a soft bulge of lower
belly that she doesn't bother
covering back up.

mom observes me from
the corner of her eye,
puckers her mouth
at my plum-stained
fingers, pulls her cardigan
tighter around herself.

harlow remains duct-taped
to my side, nudges my hands
every five minutes.

ANOTHER DINNER

marinated chicken,
garlic bread,
and caesar salad.
the meat, dairy, and starch
latch to my limbs, expand
my surface area, giving
gravity more of me
to pull down.

mom's eagle eyes watch
for me to mess up.
my fingers fumble
with the cutlery, stomach
coiling tight as a hedgehog
to protect itself. i shift
in my chair and the paper
chart in my back pocket
crinkles; a reminder.

the ghost of anna's voice
speaks in my head:
              acknowledge what you're feeling.
nervous. anxious. scared.
of the food.
of failing.

i repeat the words
of the unit's dietitian:
a calorie is a calorie is a calorie.
it still feels like a lie.

from his spot underneath
my chair, harlow groans,
demands table scraps.
i wiggle my socked feet
in the fur of his haunch.
my chair shakes as he rolls
onto his back and releases
a contented sigh.

i create my own mantra:
food becomes glucose becomes
energy becomes walks with harlow.
repeat it until my plate is empty.

BABYSITTER

do I have time to walk harlow
before you take me back?

mom's and dad's eyes lock
in silent conversation.
mom replies,
>*you have to be supervised*
>*after meals.*

please?

>*only if wren goes with you.*

across the oak table,
wren throws her head back,
like she's pleading with the gods.
>*it's cold and dark*
>*out already.*

>*then dress warm.*

wren's dramatic sigh
chafes me.
>*fine, whatever.*
>*i'll babysit.*

you're not babysitting,
i'm older than you.

a playful smile tickles
at her mouth.

> *yeah, but i'm more*
> *mature and won't go*
> *throwing up all over*
> *the neighborhood.*

.

A PLEA

it's snowing and i didn't
bring a scarf. cold
flakes fall on my
upturned face, land
light as a ladybug.
i don't wipe them away,
let them stick and melt
in chilling bites.

silence follows wren and me
for four blocks. we let
harlow's staccato sniffs
and the crunch
of boots on snow
fill the air between us.

                              i'm sorry.

wren is saturated
in the orange glow
of cloudy streetlights,
her hazel eyes fixed
on her own shuffling feet.

for what?

saying that thing about
you throwing up.
i was trying to be funny.

it was *funny.*

we lumber another three blocks.
harlow halts at a fence post,
waddles back and forth
until he's lined up, lifts
a leg, releases a stream
of yellow urine.

it's been hard
without you here.

winter seeps inside
the hood of my coat.
i scrunch my shoulders,
look at the white beneath
my boots, the yellow snow,
anywhere but at wren.

mom and dad don't
really have time for me.
they're either working
or worrying about you.

my stiff legs lock.

i'm sorry.

i'm also worried
about you. like,
you're my sister and
you're sick and i am
so scared but—

she inhales a big, snotty
breath, wipes a gloved
hand across her nose.

but i'm mad at you
for being sick.
this isn't just your life,
it's my life too.

i exhale another apology
from my numbing lips.
i'm sorry.

i know you didn't
do it on purpose.
but it doesn't
make it easier.

wren's cheeks and nose are
pink from frost, her eyelashes
coated in ice crystals, and her eyes,

too much like mom's
but completely her own,
are imploring.

> *i want my sister back.*
> *and my parents.*
> *and my life.*

i am frozen.
i don't know
what i can do.

> *try and get better.*
> *please try.*

TRYING

trying is
an earnest attempt,
like when i accept
the can of diet pop
carson offers me.
like when i sit
all afternoon
beside marianne
instead of pacing
the hallways.

trying is also
a test of how much
someone can take
before they break.
like how my stomach
is so full of carbonation
but i still eat the lentil
loaf and carrot cake
i'm given. like how
i cannot sit,
belly bursting,
and stay standing
for two and a half
hours until snack.

MONDAY WEIGH-IN

i have been
on a downward
trajectory since thursday.

i am elated.
i bite my lips to keep
from smiling.

darlene grills me.

have you been hiding food?
purging?
abusing laxatives? diuretics?

the answer to all
the questions is no.
still, i'm upped to
2700 calories.

2700

my stomach balloons
outward. after meals,
it is as dense
as a sandbag, my skin
stretched taut.
jayda gifts me an old
microwaveable heating pad,
to relax my spasming belly.

i should give up. refuse
to eat, get a feeding tube.
but wren needs me to try.

i sit at the table
for thirty minutes, an hour,
an hour and a half,
spooning morsels of meals
into my mouth, whispering
through gritted teeth
food becomes glucose becomes
energy becomes time for wren.

BRITTLE

darlene's group sessions
are the worst. full of
information packets
we read together,
darlene's monotone voice
droning on and on.

i fold and pick at
the edges of a paper
describing the dangers
of starvation on bones:
osteopenia,
kyphosis,
osteoporosis.
words i can barely
pronounce, let alone
understand.

i sigh, slump back
in my chair, and notice
nadia, usually so poised,
hunched over and gripping
her knees, her neck muscles
tight, her cords bulging.

when group ends,
nadia throws her papers
to the floor, flies off
to her room, slams
the door so hard
the whole unit shudders.

what was that?
i ask marianne,
who is unfortunate enough
to be nadia's roommate.

she shakes her head.
> *she doesn't talk about it*
> *much, but nadia was a dancer.*
> *she broke her foot during*
> *a practice or something.*
> *she had a cast*
> *when i first arrived.*

i didn't know she could dance.

jayda chimes in
from across the table.
> *she probably won't again.*
> *not professionally, anyway.*
> *who wants a ballerina*
> *with brittle bones?*

LEFT BEHIND

carson leaves on wednesday.
he and his parents have their
final discharge meeting with
dr. mantell. everyone exits
the office smiling. i can't
remember the last time
i smiled like that—
open and easy, instead
of closed and forced.

carson catches me watching
and comes over.
> hard to believe
> i'm actually leaving.

yeah.

he plops a hand on my head,
ruffles my hair like he's
petting a dog. i swat him away,
annoyed, tame my now tangled
strands while he laughs. i wonder
if this is what having an older
brother is like.

i'll follow you on insta.
feel free to message me
when you get out.
about anything, okay?

okay.
i look down
at my socked feet.
i'll miss swearing
with you at school.

       me too. even though
       you're kinda shit at it.

when he walks past the threshold
of the doors, he spins around,
flips the unit two middle fingers.
then waves an enthusiastic goodbye
to those of us left behind.

after, his old room is locked,
left empty, waiting,
for the next boy
sick enough to need it.

PERIOD

at three a.m., a dull abdominal
ache wakes me.
my underwear is moist.
i go to the bathroom,
yank my panties down,
find a gummy, brown film
coating the crotch.

i collapse in mournful
tears. this is proof i'm fat,
heavy enough that my body
bleeds again.

i seize fistfuls of rough
toilet paper, clean
the half-dried blood
clinging to my inner thighs,
stuff the rest into the lining
of my ruined underwear.
the crinkling tissue taunts
me as i tiptoe back
to bed, curl up tight
beneath the covers.

INTRUDER

my cheeks burn red
with embarrassed blood
the next morning
as nurse tammy
retrieves a bulky pack
of pads from
the med room.

they are the bad type
—thick as a diaper.

i creep around the unit,
a pariah, no longer belonging.

BURN

evening snack consists
of oatmeal cookies
and rice pudding, both
as lumpy and white
as the cellulite
on my butt. afterward,
i brush my teeth
until my mouth burns.

DECEMBER

TREE TRIMMING

the nurses decorate with
limp bows—ribbons unraveling
at the edges—and mangey
tinsel twined across every door.
they set up a tree
as thin and ragged
as the patients.

we trim the plastic pine
with paper ornaments
crafted in group therapy.
it looks absurd, like a woman
trying too hard to hide her age—
clothes too flashy,
makeup caked like flour.

FORGET

it feels wrong to watch
cartoons without carson's
high, howling laugh,
so marianne and i
relocate to the empty
tables and chairs
of the meal room
to do schoolwork.

marianne is the picture
of the perfect scholar—
focused, studious.
but i am too bloated
with thoughts of calories,
periods, body fat percentage,
and how much more of me
i have to hate.

i fidget, pace the room
one end to the other,
read all the posters about food
and eating and how i need
to keep doing it.

marianne calls me back
to our table.

> can i talk through
> this math problem with you?

i sit and listen as she
mumbles about monomials,
binomials, things i haven't
learned yet. it lulls me like
alfred's lessons do. i lose myself
in the rhythm of her voice,
forget about my body
for ten long minutes.

PLATEAU

if my weight chart
were a connect-the-dots
the past week's
plotted numbers
would draw a flat line.

when mantell calls
me into his office, i know
in my calcium-deprived bones
my calories are about to
increase. again.

it's too much already.

> *your body is telling us*
> *it's not enough.*

i could fight, scream, throw
myself on the ground
in a wild tantrum.

but what's the point?

i slump in the chair,
body numb
with senseless anger.

3000

looks like:
three slices of toast at breakfast.
an extra yogurt, juice,
or cookie with lunch.
another side of starch
with dinner. three muffins
for snack, instead of two.

3000 calories looks like
standing for an hour
after every meal, praying
this static, stoic exercise
is enough.

MESSAGE AGONY

the blinking cursor
in the empty
instagram message
mocks me. i peck out
an opening:
dear darcy.
delete.
greetings, darcy.
delete.
hi darcy.
sorry about ignoring you
for 3 months.
delete.
sorry i'm such a bad friend.
delete.
i'm sorry i haven't
written sooner.
better.

how are you?
as you know, i'm in
the hospital. a psych ward
for eating disorders.
you haven't messaged in
a while. are we still friends?

my hands tremble too
much to type. this
was a bad idea. i don't
remember how to talk
to darcy. she probably doesn't
want to hear from me
anyway. i erase my message,
bury my head in my arms.

jean's large bracelets
clatter as she sits
down beside me.
           what's going on?

i pull my hair.
*how do you speak
to someone you've avoided
for months?*

           like this.
her fingers are swift
and precise on the keyboard.
*i miss you.
i'm sorry. things have been
hard. please write back.*

i read the message
six times, reach for
jean's hand, hold it.
hit send.

ANOTHER PERIOD

a bright red splotch spreads
along marianne's leggings, plays
peekaboo as she walks ahead
of me after class. i pull her
to an alcove, whisper the
embarrassment in her ear.

i try not to recoil
when she reaches between
her legs, when her fingers
come back red.
tears drip down
her smooth black cheeks.

> *no, no, oh no, no no no.*
> *this is the first one since . . .*

me too.
it's the weight gain.
it happened
to me too.

i wrap my favorite
forest-green hoodie
around her waist,
hold her hand as we head
to the nurses' desk for pads.

255

SOLIDARITY

nadia and esther snicker,
point at my sweater
on marianne's waist.
i grit my teeth, push the fury
down, remember anna's
"let yourself feel it" advice.

this anger needs me
to do more than feel.

i need some pads too!

it comes out as a shout,
overwhelms the patients'
cruel whispers.

later, i steal cherry-scented
markers from the craft cupboard,
stay up late scribbling
puddles of red fury
on white pads.

CHERRY GRAFFITI

i inhale my breakfast
in a record fifteen minutes,
excuse myself to decorate
the unit while watchful eyes
are occupied. slap my midnight
craft experiment of colored pads
on the windows, walls, floor.
loop them around the door handles
of both nadia's, esther's rooms,
revenge for laughing
at marianne. like their bodies
were never heavy with blood.

as the nurses and patients
trickle out of the meal room,
they gasp and gag at my
menstruation decorations.
jayda whispers an astonished,
            what the actual fuck.

darlene's face purples with rage.
she dons gloves, tears
a pad off the floor with a sound
like rending duct tape.
she inhales to shout. pauses.

sniffs in. places her nose
right up to the pad and takes
one giant whiff.
unimpressed, she growls.
                    cherry.

i double over in a fit
of giggles, abdominals
throbbing with unfamiliar
laughter. darlene catches me
red-handed with marker ink.

UNEXPECTED

i'm punished with cleanup.
i rip pads up like velcro,
take pleasure as darlene
flinches at the sound.
dr. mantell wanders by.
his scalpel-gray eyes examine
my graffiti mess. a smile
tugs the corners of his stern mouth.

> *i wouldn't expect you*
> *to act out like this.*
> *good job.*

A GOOD GIRL

                    it's interesting,
anna muses, voice
drifting like she's about
to say more. i wait for her
to finish the thought
but she doesn't, only
tip-tip-tips her pen
against pursed lips.

what is?

                    your behavior.
                    usually you're so
                    rules-oriented, so
                    obedient, so . . .

good?
i offer, sitting
straighter, like
harlow waiting for
a pat on the head.
anna's pen pauses.
she turns her brown,
appraising eyes on me.

is that how you think of it?

this seems like
a trick question.
yes?

> *okay.*
> *when were other times*
> *you were "good"?*

i guess
when i get good grades.
when i behave in class.
when i do what my mom wants.
when i don't cause trouble.
when i don't complain.

> *when you do what others*
> *ask of you?*

i nod my head.

> *so, when your mom asked*
> *you to eat and you didn't,*
> *you were being bad?*

i flinch, my entire
body recoiling.

no. according to you
i was being sick.

> *were you bad when*
> *you stuck all those*
> *pads around the unit?*

that was different.
they were making fun
of marianne.

> *what about when*
> *you hid those pills?*

i didn't know anna
knew about the pills.
my mouth clenches
tight, stuck together
with wires of shame.

> *tell me evie,*
> *in all those instances,*
> *were you good*
> *or were you bad?*

GOOD GOOD GOOD

my brain repeats
while i swipe away
tears on my sweater cuff.

anna softens.
> *let's approach this*
> *another way.*
> *what do you consider*
> *bad?*

my nose is beginning
to run but if i sniff back
the snot, i'll break into sobs.

i inhale, loud,
through my mouth.
acting out.
not listening.
putting myself
or others
in danger.

wading out
too far into water
and not noticing
the risk until i am

completely submerged.

> *you've acted out*
> *with the pad stunt.*
> *you didn't listen*
> *when people said*
> *they were worried*
> *about you.*

i breathe in another
dry gasp of air.

> *and evie, you've already*
> *put yourself in so much danger.*
> *that's why you're here.*

i draw my knees
tight up into me,
press my eyes hard
against them until
i see fireworks.
reach my hands
to scratch my scalp,
but can only paw at it with
declawed fingers.

my chair tilts
to the right, and anna rubs
my back with a

eucalyptus-scented hand.

> i'm not saying you're bad
> or that you're good, just
> that you are so much more
> complicated. you are not
> only one thing. you're a
> kaleidoscope, with good
> and bad constantly shifting
> into new patterns. you understand?

i lift my head,
level anna with
an unimpressed stare.
you think i'm a crappy
plastic tube full of
broken glass.

> yes. and like that crappy tube
> you can be astonishing.
> but you need to stop letting
> who you think you should be
> get in the way of the multi-faceted
> person you are.

multi-faceted?
maybe. mostly
i feel like a big
shattered mess.

DRIFTWOOD

mantell summons me
to his office and
i brace for another
calorie increase.

> *i think you're ready*
> *for more freedoms.*

wait, what?

> *i'm taking you off close watch.*
> *you're a minor, so you can't*
> *leave the hospital grounds,*
> *but you can go off unit.*

he replaces the neon-orange
shackle on my wrist
with a laminated
white paper bracelet.

> *this is a test.*
> *abuse these freedoms*
> *and you lose them.*

this bracelet is driftwood
in the middle of the sea:
something to cling to.
a second chance.

OUTSIDE

i glide off the unit
alone for the first time
in three months, flashing
my white wristband at
everyone—a VIP going
backstage at a concert.

standing just outside the hospital
building, i let the world—the cold, gray,
snowing, traffic-congested world—
wash over me. for the first time
in years, i am not drowning.

DRAGGED DOWN

then the scale flashes
my goal weight across
its digital screen.
my vision tunnels.
the pounds wrap around me
like seaweed. drag me
down. i struggle
to keep afloat.

OBSESSIVE

i do not sit
for two days except
at mealtimes. in class
i squat on the edges of chairs
until my feet go numb.
i only sit normally
after darlene threatens
to switch my white wristband
back to orange.

"RECOVERED"

how does your goal weight feel?

terrible.

we stare at each other,
anna and i, fish tank
bubbling in the background.
she flips her wrist
in a "continue on" gesture.
terrible because . . .

i've gained all the weight
i worked so hard to lose.
i'm officially "recovered," but
all i can think about is
how i'll starve better next time.

anna promptly
interrupts.
you're not automatically recovered
once you're at a healthy weight.

aren't I?

absolutely not.

you've been here, what, three months?
serious mental illnesses take years
of consistent effort to treat.

wow, thanks,
so comforting to hear.

i'm not trying to comfort you.
i'm giving you perspective.
you can be a "healthy" weight
and still have an eating disorder.

i curl my fingers
into fists to fight
my need to scratch.
gaining weight,
being okay with it,
it's hard.

you wouldn't trust recovery
if it was easy.

MAINTENANCE

my daily calories
lower to a "maintenance level"
because my body is no longer
a gas-guzzling beater,
a neglected vehicle primed to
break down at any moment.
it is an efficient machine,
running more miles per gallon.
my joints are well-oiled,
the start-and-stop sputter
of my heart fixed.

my "healthy" body
needs my mind
to catch up.

TREE RINGS

the nurses roll out
long pages of brown
butcher's paper, make us
lie on top of them
like hunks of raw meat.
they mark our heights,
ask us to draw outlines
of what we think our bodies
look like.

i sketch myself from
the feet up—cankles,
tree-trunk legs, my ever-rising
sourdough belly, arms large
as rolled-up sleeping bags.

the sheet crinkles
as i lie down once more,
the paper offering little protection
from the leeching cold of the floor.
a nurse traces my body.
i jerk away from the ticklish
touch of her pencil,
hold back giggles
as it trails under my armpits.

the finished portrait shows
two bodies—the giant
i drew, and a slim tracing.

it's some "revealing"
lesson about fact and feeling,
actual and dysmorphic, but:
both bodies are my reality.
they are two rings
of the same tree.
two different ways
of existing at once.

i stay behind, sketch
more outlines. multiple versions
of me layered like nesting dolls.
continue until i cannot tell
the silhouettes apart.

A DATE IS SET

mantell summons me
to his office, presses
a button on his phone
as i take a seat.

> *evie's here now,*
> *mrs. anderson.*

> *hi honey!*

when i hear mom's speakerphone-
garbled voice, i snap straight
into good girl mode:
uncross my arms,
correct my posture,
replace my grimace
with the suggestion of a smile.
i hate myself for it.
hi mom.

> *as i was saying, evie's reached*
> *her goal weight and is,*
> *so far, maintaining just fine.*
> *i'm going to approve your*
> *request for her three-day*
> *pass over christmas.*

fantastic!

my exhale is long,
drawn out. i am not in trouble.
i let my shoulders slump
the tiniest bit.

> *i also wanted you both here*
> *to set a discharge date.*

the syncopated beat
of my heart throbs
in my ears.

> *i'm thinking, tentatively,*
> *january eleventh.*
> *that date is dependent*
> *on continued good behavior,*
> *particularly on this pass.*
> *how does that sound?*

mom's voice trembles.
> *that will be . . . it will be*
> *so nice to have her back home.*

finally, mantell's gray eyes
turn toward me.
> *evie?*

january 11. a date.

an actual set date.
excitement bubbles like
a baking soda volcano
in my belly. i can't believe
i'm getting out.

i'm a good girl.
i followed rules my entire
life. i can behave for
four more weeks.
yes. sounds good.

SPREADING THE NEWS

jean and alfred jump
into a jig when i tell them.
they teach marianne and me the fancy
footwork so we can join in.

on the way back
to the unit, marianne sighs.
> *first carson, now you.*
> *when's it my turn?*

jayda hugs me so hard
my bones grind
against hers.
i hug her back
just as tight.

nurse tammy gives me
a knowing wink along
with my dinner tray.

darlene inspects
my meal, points out
the dregs of milk
left behind.

your discharge is dependent
on your good behavior.
slack off and you stay.

when she turns her back,
i stick my tongue out at her.
even she can't ruin this for me.

UNYIELDING

anna teaches me
how to breathe,
tells me it will help
keep me grounded
on my three-day pass.
*i've been breathing
since i was born.*

         you do it wrong.

she directs my left hand
to my chest, my right
to the soft mound of my stomach.

         breathe from your diaphragm.
         your belly should expand
         with air when you inhale.

it's only my chest
that rises and falls.

         focus. relax your belly.

my chubby belly,
pregnant with fat.

the muscles tighten.

evie, relax.

i dig the pads of my fingers
into my unyielding abdomen,
imagine i'm popping a balloon
with every inhale.

i can't do it.

*it takes practice,
patience, and relaxation.
you'll get there.*

i prod the rigid
tissue of my belly,
doubtful.

THE HEALING GARDEN

is tucked away
on the fourth floor, just past
the cardiology unit. this atrium
ringed with green foliage,
a streaming fountain,
soft sofas speckling the floor.

in my seat beside the windows,
the magnified sunlight warms
my always-cold feet.
the babble of water lulls me
and for a minute
i do not think,
i do not worry.
i let the sun and water
and plants soothe me.
aloe vera for
my unit-scalded soul.

HEADACHES

i run into jayda outside
the elevators. she is bundled
in a wool jacket, dandelion fluff
hair hidden under a black toque,
plastic bag rustling in her hand.

you coming back from a walk too?

yes.

we fall beside each other
naturally, two sticks carried
by the same current.

hold up a minute.

she pulls a large bottle
of pills out of her bag,
nestles it in the waistband
of her too-big sweats, adjusts
the hem of her coat to cover it.
i can't even tell the pills are there.

for my headaches, remember?

i remember.
my stomach buzzes
like a disturbed wasps' nest
as we walk onto the unit.
we pass the nurses.
i don't say a word.

HUMMING

                    you look troubled,
olena says the next morning
as we stand outside
the weight room, the last
two patients in line.

i am troubled, barely
slept worrying about jayda
and the pills, mantell's
previous warning humming
around my head like a housefly:
                    let's hope your actions have no
                    future consequences.

just a bad night.

olena nods, empathetic,
and for a moment i consider
confessing everything.

but the moment passes
when jayda marches
out of the weight room,
her scowl opening into
a smile when she sees me.

CELEBRATION

jean and alfred dress up
for our last class before
the christmas break.
alfred wears a cheap, red polyester
santa suit, pompom beard hanging
on tired elastic bands.
jean dons antlers, her face made up
like a reindeer, shoulders wrapped
in a brown fur stole,
with a matching hand warmer.
the vixen to alfred's st. nick.

who would like to pet my muff?

my face blushes brighter
than alfred's too-small suit.
jean cackles with delight
as alfred, in his best santa voice, says,

oh, vixen, you ho ho ho.

jean and alfred treat
us to peppermint tea
in the cafeteria.
they gift us shiny bags
each containing sugar-free

candy, a kazoo, a container
of bubbles.

they make a scene
with their celebration—joyous
and rowdy and loud.
i tuck my chin, hide the big,
toothy smile stretching
across my face.

UNPRACTICED

dad visits wednesday afternoon.
unannounced. he's nervous
when he asks

> *do you want to go*
> *christmas shopping?*

as if he's expecting a no.

sure.

we drive to the mall, quiet as rabbits.
wander department stores full
of pastel textiles, chrome kitchenware,
the leather smell of bags, coats,
belts. i purchase gifts
for mom and wren, treats
for harlow, even a present for
dad when his back is turned.

a man ahead in line accidentally
elbows my stomach, reminds me
of my body, which now feels
far too big, too obtrusive.
christmas carols assault us
from hidden speakers,
accompanied by the sporadic

jingle of bells. the glittery
ornaments hurt my eyes,
the press of hot, hurried
human bodies crushes me.
my hairline and neck sting
with heat. my breathing
becomes shallow, rushed.

dad rests a light hand
on my shoulder.

> *it's okay. the crowd*
> *is too much for me too.*

we retreat to a corner
of the food court.
he buys us matching diet cokes,
which we sip in silence.

on the way back to the
hospital he says,

> *that was a nice afternoon,*
> *wasn't it?*

he seems so
unsure. i am too.
we are two
retired dancers trying
to remember our routine—
out of sync, stiff,

worried about disappointing
each other.
yeah.
thank you.

at the patient drop-off,
he leans over the seat
and hugs me. it's like
writing with my left hand
—unnatural, unpracticed.

his watchful eyes burn
the back of my neck
as i walk into the building.
i turn around once i'm inside,
wave at him through glass doors
as he drives away.

A REAL TREAT

darlene pounces
on the shopping bags
the moment i walk in.
plastic crinkles as she paws
through with leathery hands,
her eyes shining with delight
when she finds the treats
i bought for harlow.

prohibited.
i'm confiscating these.

dog treats?

outside food.
we can't have patients
bingeing.

is she shitting me?
i'm not going
to eat dog treats.

temptation comes
in many forms.

i put on my best
good girl smile,
sweet as cotton candy.
curtsy with a flourish.
thank you, darlene.
how would we ever survive
without you and your infinite wisdom?

nurse tammy belly-laughs
as i shuffle backward
to my room.

THRUMMING

my packed bag rests
by my feet in the hall.
my nerves are thrumming
wires of displaced electricity.
i pace in tight lines,
try to work off this
anxious energy.

jayda groans.
          you're making me dizzy.

i join her leaning,
aloof, against the wall.
you'll be just as restless
when your husband
comes tomorrow.

her laugh is bitter.
          right. for my oh so generous
          one night pass. thanks, mantell.

mom barrels onto the unit,
boots clunking like a train
engine. her eyes flit between
jayda and me, mouth dropping

in displeasure. i pretend not
to notice, turn to jayda
and wrap her in a hug.
see you on the twenty-seventh.

have a good pass.

she clings to me
a moment too long.
i'm the one that breaks
away first.

CHRISTMAS EVE

before, we'd decorate
the tree together while squares
of caramel fudge melted into puddles
of sugar on our tongues.

before, relatives arrived in droves
for a christmas feast:
turkey, stuffing, mashed potatoes,
gravy, green beans, cranberries, corn,
bread rolls, cheesy broccoli casserole,
full-sugar pop, eggnog, gingerbread,
butter tarts, brownies, shortbread, trifle.

thank god we're done
with before.

the tree is already decorated,
presents strewn beneath,
harlow sniffing them, suspicious.
mom still insists on a traditional
christmas dinner, for the four of us.

only my parents are there
to watch me dish up food.
one slice of white turkey,

one roll, half a cup of mashed
potatoes, one teaspoon of gravy,
one cup of corn, quarter cup
of broccoli casserole.

my plate is a portrait
of precision. control.

across the table, wren
drowns her food under
a flood of gravy.
i push a couple kernels
of corn into my potatoes,
scoop the mixed food into
my mouth. it's not bad, but
not particularly good, either.
just different.

THE ONLY WAY

buttermilk pancakes doused
in syrup are a christmas morning
tradition. i expected them.
i am still not prepared.

the kitchen smells
sticky with maple.
                    it smells like hell.

i want to gorge myself
on pancakes.
                    i'd rather starve.

mom sets a plate of three
average-sized pancakes
in front of me—pat of butter
on top, no whipped cream,
three tablespoons of syrup
in a bowl on the side.

she says,
        i calculated the amount you'd need.
        to make it easier.

anger coils in my chest,
ready to spew venomous
words from my throat,
yell about boundaries,
overstepping,
        except

mom's pale brow is crinkled,
her smile small, subdued.
nervous?

the offending
pancakes become
care and concern. perhaps
she is loving me in
the only way
she knows how.

i inhale three deep breaths,
from my belly like anna
taught, quell my snake-like rage.
pick up my knife, spread butter
across the doughy circles.
thanks, mom. this helps.

TAKING UP

on my final morning, harlow
and i trod through a field
of untouched snow, stamp
our footprints everywhere.

he drops to his back, rolls
an abstract imprint of himself
into the powder. i lie down too,
arms and legs splayed like a star,
swipe them back and forth—
a lopsided snow angel.
a small, temporary sign
that my body took up space.

i consider destroying
the angel. too imperfect,
too large. but then harlow
barks, tugs at his leash.
i decide, half-hearted,
to let it be.

we walk, snow-damp,
back toward home,
where i'll be loaded
into the car
and driven to the unit
in time for snack.

MISSING

jayda is not at breakfast.
everyone attends breakfast.
it's a rule.

i creep down the hall
to her bedroom.
knock on the open door.
jayda?

behind me kristy says,

                she's not back yet, evie.

i startle, turn around.
her pass was only
until the twenty-sixth.

her smiling face turns
somber and smooth
like a perfectly ironed
linen napkin.

                no one told you.

told me what?

                she's in the er.
                she overdosed last night.

SINKING

i'm drowning.

hands gone cold and numb,
feet stuck fast. my vision
muddies and the door,
walls, kristy, blur.
my body sways
with the current.

kristy's voice is muffled
by thick water. she leaves,
returns with nurse tammy,
who grabs my arm,
wrenches me out,
brings me to shore.

MY FAULT

she tried to kill herself
because i got a longer pass
than she did.

she tried to kill herself
because i'm getting discharged
before her.

she tried to kill herself
with the pills
i kept secret.

she tried to kill herself
because of
me.

BLAME

my stomach is glutted
with guilt. i substitute
all my meals for strawberry-
flavored ensure. the taste
of perfumed metal drips
down like paint, colors
my insides coral pink.

between liquid meals,
i lie motionless in bed,
dream of riptides
dragging me out to sea.

ALL I DESERVE

darlene stomps
into my room, barks
at me like a drill sergeant.

*are you just going
to lie there moping?*

i tunnel further
into my blankets,
away from her anger.

*this kind of conduct
helps no one.*

pull the comforter
over my head
to hide my
sorry face.

*we expect better from patients
this close to discharge.*

breathe in the hot,
stale blanket air.

you can't let jayda's choices
affect your own.

hum in the back
of my throat to drown
out the voices, darlene's
and the one in my head—
the one telling me
this pain
is all i deserve.

ADMISSION

if i don't say something
the pressure of my guilt
will kill me. but speaking it out
loud might kill me too.

my body can't get
warm. i tilt
on my axis from too
many days in bed.

> get up.
> the pity party is over.

the blanket is ripped
away. i whimper. pathetic.
lift my heavy head and find
anna standing at the foot
of my bed, blanket in hand.

i thought you were
off for the holidays.

> so did i, but darlene called.
> said it was an emergency.

oh.

        why are you sabotaging yourself
        so close to discharge?

the truth leaks out like pus.
i knew about jayda's pills
and i didn't tell anyone.

anna sits.
the bed droops
under her weight.
she is close enough that
her heat radiates.
        evie, what jayda did
        was not your fault.

i curl up my body
as small as it will go.

        evie. look at me.

i do and her eyes
are certain.

        this was not your fault.

anna would never
lie to me, but

i could have done something.

> *like what? you're fourteen.*
> *if jayda wants to die, there's*
> *nothing you nor i nor a team*
> *of doctors could do to stop her.*

knowing that hurts.
i reply with another
pitiful whine.

she jumps off the bed,
opens my closet, and digs
out my jacket, mittens, hat.

> *get dressed.*
> *we're going on a field trip.*

PLATES

we end up outside
an empty loading dock.
the cold air freezes
my nose hair. i shuffle
from left foot to right.

anna pulls a stack
of plates and a black marker
from her tote bag.

> *i want you to write down*
> *what's hurting you. could be recent,*
> *could be from a while ago, i don't care.*
> *write your pain on these plates.*

this is the stupidest thing
she has ever asked of me.
but i do it.
with frozen fingers,
i write stiff and slow.
a fawn taking her first steps.

"ignored me"
"were never home"
"left me at the hospital"

something in my core
kicks. the thing i have fought
to swallow, ignore,
starve.
the rotten center
of my body, the pith,
the scared little girl
drowning in a lake,
wondering if anyone
is coming to save her.

her fear burns.
it is infection. it is fever.
it is a necrotic wound roaring
for acknowledgment. i place the marker
in that little girl's hand, help her
write our pain.
so much pain i worry
the plates will run out.

> "didn't notice i was sick"
> "too focused on me being sick"
> "stopped messaging"
> "asked me to hide your meds"
> "made me drink ensure"
> "made me eat trigger foods"
> "upped my calories"
> "tried to kill yourself"
> "almost let me drown"

when i'm done,
anna says,

        smash them.

uncertain, i toss
the first plate.
it barely breaks,
a hairline fracture.

        come on, evie,
        you're angrier than that.

and i am.
i am so angry.
i clutch that younger evie
close, let her anger catch,
let her wildfire tantrum
blaze through me.

the second plate
smashes so hard, bits turn
to dust. i grab another.
and another. let myself be
ravaged by starving rage.

when the last plate shatters
on icy pavement, i scream.
i scream for that little girl.

i scream loud enough for her
to know i'm coming.
she screams with me.

i sob.

anna holds me
until i am ready
to breathe.

BREAKING

after we've picked up
the porcelain pieces of my pain,
anna and I retreat to her office
and the gurgle of her fish tank.

we review my self-care chart:
> go for a walk
> pet harlow
> journal
> destroy a crayon
> talk to someone
> let myself feel
> breathe

> *no more holding in your emotions.*
> *you're not a plate, evie.*
> *you can't keep breaking.*

THINGS I HAVE BROKEN

the skin of my head
my friendship with darcy
my ability to feel hunger
my parents' trust
my body

half a box of crayons
my loneliness
my starvation
my parents' expectations
my pain

the surface of my own
suffocating perfection

TRY AGAIN

i eat dinner, even though
my stomach is still queasy.
even though jayda
is still not here. i down
my glass of milk, ingest
my steamed broccoli
and cauliflower, butter
and chew my whole wheat
bun, cut slivers of a seasoned
chicken breast, eat methodical
forkfuls of vanilla cake—
sickening icing first.

after, darlene lifts the plates
and cutlery to check
i have not hidden anything.

> *so you've decided*
> *to behave again.*

if i were a porcupine,
my quills would fan out
in warning.
i ignore that instinct.
thank you for calling anna.

just doing my job.

an unflattering snort
of laughter escapes,
which i quickly hide
with a cough.
leave it to darlene
to take my olive branch
and burn it.

TIRED

a young man arrives to take
up residence in carson's old room.
his neon-green hair reflects
off his pale skin, making him
appear perpetually seasick.

he does not look scared
like i was when i arrived.
he looks tired.

i'm tired too.
exhausted from the effort
it takes to stay sick.
i want to let my body rest,
for a little while, at least.

REBUILDING

darcy messages back
and the muscle in my chest
that i didn't know was clenched
releases.

hi evie.
i miss u too.
i'm srry things have
been hard. want to
come over when
ur back and
talk about it?

i remember
the popcorn,
candy, slushies
fast food that is
always present
when i hang out
with darcy.

i type out
an immediate reply.
i can't come over.
i'll phone

you instead.
stare at the screen.
delete.
retype.
i'm home in two weeks.
i'll see you then.

WHEN JAYDA RETURNS

she looks brittle
and worn like my old
swing set back home.

sits at the edges of
the meal room, a feeding
tube running up her nose,
siphoning ensure into her stomach.

i ache to rush to her, hug her,
talk to her. but the inward
curve of her spine, round
and guarded like a pill bug,
says to leave her alone.

and what would i say?
thank god you're okay.
i was worried.
i'm sorry.

are we still friends?
were we ever friends?
or were we both just sick?

i smile at her as i walk past.
her eyes remain fixed on the floor.

JANUARY

JANUARY 1

it should be like every
other morning from
the past four months.

except, breakfast is buttermilk
pancakes drizzled in sticky maple
syrup. i savor it, eyes closed
and grateful. when the guilt
of enjoying food slinks
in on soft-padded feet,
i do not let it consume me.

RECOVERY DEFINITIONS

food—
        energy for:
        playing with harlow,
        being a better sister to wren,
        a thinking brain,
        a beating heart.

trigger—
        still:
        fatty food, sugary food,
        models, instagram, fat bodies,
        slim bodies, medium bodies,
        any body, the number on the scale,
        the number of steps taken,
        the number on a food label,
        the number on my clothes.
        maybe always. hopefully not.

healthy—
        taking care of myself.

disciplined—
        eating.

beautiful—
    a box of unopened crayons.

enough—
    what i'm learning to be.

5 DAYS

12000 calories—
2400 calories a day
until i leave.
then i'm gone.

KEEP IN TOUCH

marianne and i spend
my last sunday
in the patient lounge,
a superhero movie
blaring from the tv.
when the older patients
try to come in, we both shout
teens only!
double over
in rippling laughs.

i got my discharge date,
marianne announces.
*february third. just over
a month away.*

congrats!

she grins, twists
a braid with nervous fingers.
*we'll keep in touch, right?
when we're both gone?*

yeah, of course.

she exhales relief,
gestures vaguely
at the walls around us.

> *i think it'll help, having someone*
> *to talk to that gets*
> *all of this.*

even though we're leaving,
neither of us is getting
over "all of this,"
over the unit,
anytime soon.

A PLAN

how does it feel?

terrifying.
i thought i would
be more ready.

ready how?

happier. not scared
of gaining. confident
i can make myself eat.

anna sets aside
her always present,
always scribbling pen.

evie, i've worked on this unit
for ten years. none of my patients
have ever felt ready.
i don't know if you're ready.
i hope you are.

if i'm not?

i'm still here. we'll continue
our weekly meetings.
we have a plan to support you.

it's more than i had before.

A TINY MOMENT

i sit with jean and alfred
on short plastic chairs,
a goodbye too big to swallow
floating between us.

alfred breaks our silence.

> *we got you a going*
> *away present.*

jean hands me a plain
white book, with a black-and-white
photo of a bird feeding
from a spoon on the cover.

devotions *by mary oliver?*

> *her poems will bring you hope*
> *on hard days.*

the spine cracks open
and the pages smell of glue.
jean's and alfred's names
and emails are scrawled
across the first page.

tears wet my face.
thank you.
i don't think i could have
survived this place
without you two.

they embrace me in
a claustrophobic hug, my neck
tilted at a painful angle, alfred's
mustache tickling my cheek.
for a tiny moment
my entire stomach
relaxes.

jean mumbles in my ear,

> *don't you dare come back,*
> *you darling girl.*

FINAL MORNING

somehow,
i pack all evidence
of my four-month stay
in one suitcase.

my side of the room
lies empty,
no longer mine.
it belongs to the endless
parade of the starving—
and i am ready to eat.

BRANDED

i take one final walk
around the unit, brand my brain with
the beep of the scale at weigh-in,
the scent of saline solution,
the shuffle of patients' pacing,
the oppressive fluorescent lights,
the clunk of metal doors.
these awful memories
will keep me well.

DEFLATED

i stop outside jayda's open door—
she has lost the privilege of
the unit's pretend privacy.
a low, murmuring voice drifts
from inside. i knock on
the doorframe.

yes?

inside, jayda sits in bed,
the head propped up
to support her. an iv
and ng tube wind down
and into her, the attached
machines beating opposing
rhythms as they pump
jayda full of a cocktail
of calories and medication.
she is so deathly white
i can see the criss-crossing
blue of her veins.

also attached to her is a man,
tall and bearded, grasping
her left hand in both of his.

her husband.
he speaks again.
                    hello. who are you?

i'm evie,
i respond, expecting
my name to mean something.
he stares at me blankly.

umm, i came to check on you,
jayda. to see how you're doing
before i . . .
i can't say it. it feels cruel
that i'm leaving
and she's still stuck here.

we stare at each other
and i'm reminded
of my sixth birthday,
when my parents bought me
a foil princess balloon
as big as i was.
i dragged the balloon
everywhere before
it began deflating,
the princess floating lower
and lower before she
collapsed.

jayda looks like that balloon:
crumpled, low.

i just wanted to thank you
for making me feel
less alone.

jayda's eyes well up.
she turns away from me,
wipes her tears with
the corner of a hospital
blanket. she never brought
her own, said she didn't
want to make the unit
feel like home.

sorry to disturb you.
i scurry out of the room
so jayda doesn't
see me cry.

MENDING

my family arrives
just on time for
the discharge meeting,
prepared to bring back the evie
they dropped off in september.

but that evie didn't know about units
for people who don't eat,
couldn't calculate the exact
amount of ensure needed
to replace an oreo.
she had no idea about
feeding tubes,
cleaning blood,
attempted suicide,
how to smash plates.

the girl they're bringing
home is a girl half-mended
        and healing.

SISTER

mantell opens his office door
for the discharge meeting.

i raise a hand
that's itching to scratch
my worries into my head.
instead, wren grasps it
within her cool,
cupped fingers.

she's grown at least
an inch taller and her eyes,
those hazel eyes,
are level with my own.

i grip her palm with my one
hand, and with the other i clutch
the cobalt crayon hidden
in my pocket, inhale through
my nose, then march
into the office.

MY PSYCHIATRIST

DR. MANTELL,
his nameplate
shouts.
i fight the urge
to shout his name
right back at him.
sit up in my chair.

my gaze washes over
his thinning hair, the fine
wrinkles spiderwebbing
at the edges of his eyes.

evie.

i meet his stare.
dr. mantell.

a giant grin
spreads across his face.
let's discuss why we're all here.

RELEASE

as i leave mantell's office,
i rip off my white manacle
and toss it in the trash.

the scrutinizing eyes of
the other patients stick to me
like burrs and prickle
on the back of my neck
as i pick up my suitcase.

i walk over to marianne,
press a paper with my
cell phone number
into her palm.
she pulls me in
for a hug, whispers,

good luck.

i turn, exit the unit doors
for what i hope
is the last time.

FLOATING

i am in the car, sandwiched
between dread and hope
as the hospital disappears.
my heart thrashes at its loss,
breath tightens in my lungs,
and i am five again, flailing
in an uncaring lake.

except my feet
are not buried in mud.
my head is not
underwater, and
i know how to swim.

i stretch out my arms, my legs,
take up the space my body needs,
        and float.

ACKNOWLEDGMENTS

Thank you to my agent, Ismita Hussain. From the beginning, you were the champion Evie and I needed. Thank you for your patience, your empathy, and your belief. Additional thanks to Gabriella Melendez for reading and loving an early version of this book, and to the rest of the team at Great Dog Literary.

To my editor, Lauri Hornik: I am grateful every day that my book found its home with you. Rocky Pond is truly special, and I know it will help many children and teens feel less alone. Thank you to Regina Castillo, who saved me from typos and incorrectly typed em-dashes. Liz Montoya Vaughan, thank you for all your efforts promoting my book. Thanks to Sylvia Bi for my book interiors, Kaitlin Yang for my cover design, and Holly Stapleton for the breathtaking cover art. And all my gratitude and praise to the amazing team at Penguin Teen.

Rayanne Haines, my friend and mentor—this book would be a 555-page mess without you. Thank you for your edits and your fierce poetry. Thanks as well to the Writers' Guild of Alberta Mentorship Program for connecting me and Rayanne. To Maria, Sylvia, and Joni—my Humber Writing Cohort—I see your influences fingerprinted everywhere in this book; our little poetry group is a gift. Geoffrey Manderscheid and Kathleen Bell, thank you for trusting me with the St. Albert Poet Laureate role. You two have opened doors for me. I doubt I'll ever be able to repay you.

Of course, I must thank Gail Sidonie Šobat and Frank Elliott, my teachers, mentors, and friends. You two brought color back to my life; I would not have survived hospitalization without you both. An extra thanks to Gail, who gave me and countless teens a haven in YouthWrite.

All my love to my mom and dad, whom I have put through too much. I couldn't see it back then, but you two saved my life. Patrick, Taylor, and Rachel—I adore being your sister. Thanks for putting up with my plethora of "quirks." To Danielle, my oldest friend and most enthusiastic supporter, sorry I made you cry at yoga class (but thank you for caring for me that much). Diana, your near-weekly hospital visits were a balm. Thanks for getting me the most inappropriate X-Men comic instead of a card. Kaleigh and Maximus, the two dogs who inspired Harlow, thank you for teaching me I am worth loving. Thank you to all my friends and family, too numerous to name, who continue supporting me wholeheartedly.

I would be remiss not to give thanks to all the therapists, doctors, nurses, and health care professionals who have cared for me over the years. You've all kept me alive, despite some pretty terrible odds.

Mike. How did I get lucky enough to be loved by you? Thank you for everything, but especially the book title. (P.S. I'm still really into you).

Lastly, I thank you, dear reader. Whether you relate to Evie's struggles or not, know you are worthy of love, from others and yourself.

RESOURCES

Admitting you need help is never easy, but it is always brave. If you are struggling with disordered eating and mental health challenges, please reach out to the following support systems:

- The National Eating Disorders Association (NEDA): www.nationaleatingdisorders.org
- The Crisis Text Line: crisistextline.org; Text 741741
- 988 Suicide Crisis Hotline: chat online at 988lifeline.org; call or text 988

If, like the author, you live in Canada, you can access these support systems:

- The National Eating Disorder Information Centre (NEDIC): visit www.nedic.ca to chat online; call 1-866-633-4220
- 988 Suicide Crisis Helpline: call or text 988